MINI MIRACLES

THE CHURCH DOGS OF CHARLESTON #1

MELISSA STORM

© 2018, Melissa Storm

All rights reserved. Except as permitted under the U.S. Copyright Act of 1976, no part of this publication may be reproduced, distributed or transmitted in any form or by any means, or stored in a database or retrieval system without the prior written permission of the publisher.

Editor: Megan Harris
Cover & Graphics Designer: Mallory Rock
Proofreader: Falcon Storm & Jasmine Bryner

This is a work of fiction. Names, characters, organizations, places, events, and incidents are either products of the author's imagination or are used fictitiously. Any resemblance to actual persons, living or dead, or actual events is purely coincidental.

No part of this work may be reproduced, or stored in a retrieval system, or transmitted in any form or by any means, electronic, mechanical, photocopying, recording, or otherwise, without written permission of the publisher.

Partridge & Pear Press
PO Box 72
Brighton, MI 48116

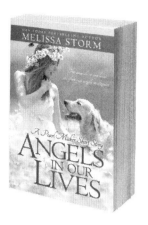

A FREE GIFT FOR YOU!

Thank you for picking up your copy of *Mini Miracles*. I so hope you love it! As a thank-you, I'd like to offer you a free gift. That's right, I've written a short story that's available exclusively to my newsletter subscribers. You'll receive the free story by e-mail as soon as you sign up at www.MelStorm.com/Gift. I hope you'll enjoy both stories. Happy reading!

MELISSA S.

To Sky Princess and Mila:
My own personal Chihuahua miracles

PROLOGUE

PASTOR ADAM

Some say that whenever it snows in Charleston, God is giving a miracle to His most favorite of places. I tried to remember that as the cold reaching fingers of the wind poked and prodded my cheeks, nose, and everything else not already covered up by my scratchy winter getup.

But the more I tried to be optimistic about the shocking turn in the weather forecast, the harder that miraculous snow swirled. Soon it had bleached out the entire sky so that it was hard to tell where earth ended and the heavens began. We had a veritable snow storm on our hands just in time for the celebration of His birth.

I mumbled a quick prayer that those traveling tonight would remain safe and hugged my threadbare coat tighter around my shoulders. Head down, I fought against the wind, marching ever closer toward my destination.

Leave it to me to get so caught up in my Christmas Eve sermon that I'd forget my cell phone right there on the pulpit! Lucky thing I did, though, because as I finally reached the front doors of the sanctuary, I discovered a most disturbing sight.

Our locally famous nativity scene had been on the fritz all week, but now the angels' glowing halos had plum run out of power, casting the entire display into darkness. And on Christmas Eve, no less.

Ignoring the cold, which had found its way straight up underneath my clothes, I stepped closer to investigate the source of our power outage. Last summer old Mrs. Clementine had taken it upon herself to plant a little garden right outside the church. How could I say no to her request when she said all the food from our newly christened vegetable patch would be donated to feed the hungry?

And so with more than a little trepidation, I said *yes*, and unfortunately so did every little critter within a twenty mile radius. Even with the crops resting for the winter, I had no doubt that one of Mrs. Clementine's rabbit friends had tried to make a home of Christ's manger—and a snack of His power cords.

Upon closer inspection, I found that—yes, just as I'd suspected—a tiny ball of brown fluff had nestled into the nativity right there between Mary, Joseph, and the kindly shepherds who'd come to pay their respects.

Darn varmits!

Well, that's what I wanted to think, but then I stopped myself. These poor creatures hadn't expected the sudden snowfall either. They just wanted to get warm, and maybe God had sent me back to offer assistance on His behalf.

My toes began to go numb, but I tried to ignore that tingly sharpness as I stepped in for a closer look at the trembling animal.

Imagine my surprise when I found not just one creature, but five!

Right there next to the little Lord Jesus lay a mother dog and her four newborn pups. How they'd managed to survive this long was truly by the grace of God.

I didn't want to leave them, but I couldn't carry them all at once either. At least not on my own. After retrieving the box that our latest batch of hymnals had arrived packed inside, I stripped off my scarf and made a little nest. Then one by one, I lifted the mama and her puppies into the cardboard carrier and brought them into our church to get warm.

My lungs could scarcely take in a single breath of air until I made sure that each pup was alive and well. Only by the glory of God each of these tiny newborns moved just enough to show me they were okay. You must understand these dogs were hardly bigger than my own thumb. They could have easily been mistaken for rat pups if not for that brave mama dog.

A quick search on my newly retrieved phone confirmed that these were not just any dogs. They were the most diminutive of all dog breeds.

I didn't even stop to question why the Almighty had sent me five Chihuahuas in need as an early gift for His birthday. I didn't have to, because right then I knew beyond the shadow of any doubt these dogs were meant to find us. Surviving that cold Christmas Eve outdoors was only the first of many miracles that mama dog and her pup would bring to our congregation…

CHAPTER 1

ABIGAIL

Abigail Sutton sat in the dark living room waiting for her father to return from his Christmas Eve sermon. Much to his chagrin, she'd refused to attend church with him that evening. She also wouldn't go tomorrow morning, next Sunday, or any other day for the rest of her life as long as she could avoid it.

Avoiding church when your father was the pastor took quite some effort, but Abigail had committed herself to just that. The last time she'd stepped foot into the Eternal Grace sanctuary had been for her husband's funeral, which had forever tainted the place as far as she was concerned.

It had destroyed her relationship with God, too.

She'd happily praised His name all her life, and for what? The first time she'd truly needed God, He'd failed to show up. What good is having an all-powerful Heavenly Father if he couldn't even take the one second that was needed to shield her husband from the bomb blast that had claimed him far too soon?

Then there was the guilt.

Abigail herself had been the one to convince Owen to take a second tour of duty before they'd settle down to start their family. If she'd just asked him to stay home, they'd be together singing holiday hymns at church with her father and planning the start of their family side by side, hand in hand.

Instead, Abigail sat alone. She'd moved back in with her father about two months ago. Back to her childhood home in Charleston.

It was an odd thing returning to your hometown when you thought you'd already left it behind. It was almost as if her life with Owen hadn't even happened, like the world wasn't just burying his body but also his memory. But it couldn't get rid of her husband that easily, for Abigail still had two very good reminders.

One was the glistening gold band on her finger.

They said people wore rings on their second smallest finger because it had a vein linked straight to the heart. She'd always liked that.

Her other reminder of Owen was also near to her heart, as in literally growing just beneath it. Their child. The last piece of Owen anyone would ever have in this world.

She didn't know how to feel about becoming a mother and a widow at almost the exact same time. She'd only found out about her pregnancy a few weeks before the solider with downcast eyes and a blank expression had delivered the folded flag to her doorstep. She'd called to tell Owen the news even though it was still early, and conventional wisdom said not to tell anyone until the first "dangerous" twelve weeks had passed.

But the news of their child was supposed to keep him safe, give him something that much more special to which he'd returned. Instead, she would always have to wonder if it had been the distraction that knocked him off his game and ultimately ended his life way out there in that horrible desert so far from home.

She hated picturing it, but she couldn't stop either. Every time Abigail closed her eyes, she saw her

Owen smiling and wiping away tears of joy at their wedding. But in an instant, his handsome face would be replaced by a bloodied, torn visage mangled by pain. It was this last haunting version of Owen that remained with her, and it didn't even look like him.

But what about their baby? If it turned out to be a boy, would it look like Owen? The *real* Owen?

She didn't know whether that would make things easier or not. Would having a little boy the spitting image of his father break her heart every time she looked at him—or would it soothe her?

Abigail wished she didn't have to consider these things. She wished she could be a normal mother expecting her first child and expecting her husband home healthy, happy, and in time for dinner.

A part of her also wished that she had never met Owen at all. Each time Abigail thought this, though, a tremendous wave of guilt overtook her.

When would the tears stop coming? When would the guilt stop eating her from the inside out? When would she actually be happy about this baby?

Never couldn't possibly be the answer, but it was the one she expected. She'd given God her everything, only for Him to take it all away at the first chance He got.

She glanced at the clock on her cell phone. Her

father should have been home at least half an hour ago. She groaned and curled her legs up beneath her on the chair. It wasn't that she needed his company, but she liked to have benchmarks by which she could measure the passage of time.

Her biggest comfort these days was simply that time pressed ever onward. After all, it was supposed to heal all wounds. And Abigail had few other options left when it came to finding some way—any way—to begin to feel normal again.

Another five minutes passed before she heard the sound of her father fiddling with the doorknob outside. "Abigail, can you help?" he called through the thick wooden door. "I have a surprise!"

Slowly, she lifted herself from the chair, bracing herself for whatever came next. She'd asked him not to make a big fuss of Christmas this year, but that didn't mean he'd chosen to listen. Her sweet father was always coming up with grand schemes, and they all too often involved her. Even before Abigail had moved back home, he'd often call her out of the blue and stop by the base to invite her on an impromptu day trip.

Normally she loved his zeal for life, but lately it was just too much. She needed him to be calm, reserved, forgettable. Then maybe she could put these painful days of grieving behind her, too.

Somehow she doubted that would happen. She took a deep breath, then placed a shaking hand on the door knob and twisted it open. The surprise that greeted her on the doorstep was quite possibly the last thing she'd ever have expected…

CHAPTER 2
ABIGAIL

Abigail took a step back as her father rushed past her into the house. In his arms he carried an old cardboard box. He'd taken off his coat and flung it over the top so that she couldn't see what was inside.

She heard it, though—a mix of whimpers and squeaks that surely meant they were in for a calamitous holiday.

"Oh no." Abigail gave her father a stern look. "Did a squirrel have babies in the attic again? You know you don't have the time to look after them. You were too upset last time when—"

"Yes, I know what happened last time." Her father turned to her with a huge grin on his wind-chapped face. "But this time will be different."

She gave him a fatigued sigh. She hated to dampen his spirits, but she just didn't have the energy for yet another ill-fated rescue attempts. "Different how?"

"Well, they aren't squirrels, and I'm not raising them." His eyes glowed like the beginning sparks of a fire. There was no stopping him now. "You are," he concluded with an enormous Cheshire grin.

Abigail wanted to argue that she didn't have a maternal bone in her body, but the baby growing inside her seemed to imply otherwise.

"Take a look," he said, setting the box on the carpeted floor and finally raising his coat to offer her a peek inside.

"Puppies!" she shouted, eyeing the wriggling balls of pink, black, and brown with hesitation. "Where did you get a box of puppies? And *how* when you were supposed to be giving the Christmas Eve sermon?"

He waved his hand dismissively. "This happened after."

Abigail slowly approached and let the mother dog sniff her hand. She was half fawn colored and half white with giant ears flanking either side of her head. She looked from her nursing pups to Abigail and squinted before letting out a tremor that shook her whole body.

"Oh my gosh!" Abigail cried. "Is she okay?"

"That's Mama Mary, and she'll be just fine. She got her babies to safety. I found them cuddled in the manger right next to the little Lord Jesus himself."

"I suppose that's why you named her Mama Mary," Abigail said with a smirk. Even her cold, dead heart warmed a bit to the sweet puppies and their heroic mother. "And there are four puppies. Did you name them after the four gospels?"

He laughed as they both stood transfixed by the squirming pups before them. "They don't have names yet, although that isn't a bad idea. I figured we'd let the Sunday school kids bestow the honor."

"Wait, does that mean you're planning to keep them?" She glanced to her father in shock. While he'd always loved all of God's creatures, he'd never exactly been a pet person. What had happened with the squirrels several years ago had been quite the anomaly—and she thought they'd all learned their lesson from it.

When a sheepish grin lit her father's face, she knew there was no way she'd be able to convince him to take the dogs to a shelter.

"I thought they could be a Christmas gift. The

fact they found us in that storm has got to be a sign. This isn't just one miracle—it's a whole litter."

"And Mama Mary makes five. Five dogs!" She wanted to be supportive, but someone needed to be realistic here. "How on earth are we going to give a proper home to five dogs?" she demanded.

Her father was completely nonplussed by Abigail's attempts to protest. He simply smiled and pointed above. "The Lord will provide a way," he said.

"You always say that."

"It's always true."

Abigail hid the smile that tried to creep across her normally placid face. If nothing else, her father was consistent, and that was something she'd always found comforting. In that way, it was nice to be home. She should be grateful that she at least had a loving home to return to. It was hard to imagine things could be worse, but of course they always could.

These nearly frozen over pupsicles were proof enough of that.

"You know we at least have to look for the owners," she pointed out softly.

"I know that, but I also know nothing will come of it. I prayed a lot on the drive over. God wanted us to have these dogs. That's why He sent them." He rubbed his hands and blew air into them, then let them hover over the pups, using this makeshift heater to warm them further.

So God saw to it that these five dogs were saved, but my husband wasn't important enough to warrant his attention? Abigail thought bitterly, hating herself as she did. She should be happy that the little animals hadn't caught their deaths outside, not jealous.

Not angry.

She'd never been like that before, and she didn't want to be like that now. "Maybe you're right, but we still owe it to…" She hesitated. "To, uh, Mama Mary and her children to at least try."

"I agree," he answered simply. "This won't be like the time with the squirrels," he added as an afterthought.

Oh, those darned squirrels… Truth be told, she liked the puppies better already, but she would keep that to herself.

CHAPTER 3

ABIGAIL

After moving the box from the table to the floor, Abigail sat with the dogs while her father zipped around the house procuring arrangements for them. An old pillow with an even older throw blanket draped on top became their bed, a pair of ceramic cereal bowls converted into food and water dishes, and a space heater set atop an overturned milk crate helped to warm the area.

"Now I'm going to make Mama Mary a dinner like she's never had before," he said, kneeling down to scratch the dog between its ears before popping back up and heading toward the kitchen.

"Don't tell me you're planning to feed her the Christmas ham," Abigail called after him, half-believing he would.

His laughter floated over from the stove. "No, that would take too long. But I figure our good girl has earned herself a nice New York strip."

The mother Chihuahua grunted in affirmation, and Abigail could swear she heard the dog's belly rumble. She couldn't stop the chuckle that bubbled to the surface. It felt both amazing and like the worst kind of betrayal to Owen's memory. This was far too soon for her to be happy over something so trivial.

She grew silent as she watched the little puppies nurse at their mama's side. While they squirmed and whined freely, the mother dog stayed mostly still and quiet—like Abigail herself. The last thing she needed was to get attached to a sick dog, only to have it die before the morning sun.

"I think we need to take them in to see a vet," she called to her father.

He answered back after a series of three loud plops and sizzles that told her he was making steaks for more than just the one of them. "I called around, but no one's open tonight or tomorrow."

She tried to think, at last remembering who it was they knew for this kind of thing. "What about Mr. Manganiello? Doesn't he work with animals?"

"He's celebrating Christmas with his family same

as everyone else. Besides, we've got this. You and me, just like the old days."

Ah, the old days… back when Abigail's biggest problem had been whether or not she could convince her father to let her attend the freshman dance with dreamy Gavin Holbrook as her date. After much pleading he'd said yes, but only on the condition that he could chaperone. Abigail had never been so mortified in her entire life, but that hadn't stopped Gavin from sneaking a kiss on the front doorstep before they'd said goodnight.

How long ago that seemed. She'd lived and died many times in the decade and a half between ninth grade and the new, sadder life she struggled through now. Each day was a gift, that's what she'd believed before. These days, she knew better.

And yet…

Her heart would break all over again if this poor mother dog didn't live to see her puppies grow into strong, full-grown ankle biters. Abigail didn't know much about dogs, but she knew enough to know that Chihuahuas were fierce, yappy little things.

Why couldn't her father have found a litter of Golden Retriever puppies instead?

Guilt hardened in her stomach once more as

Abigail watched Mama Mary breathe heavily and close her eyes.

"Hey, hey," she said gently, nudging the dog until it opened its eyes again. "We're going to get through this. Don't give up."

She continued to stroke the dog's patchy fur and murmur to it while her father prepared their dinners. Judging from the poor thing's condition, she'd either never had an owner or had been missing for a very long time. What if her owner had been searching for her all this time? What if the dog had finally found help for her puppies but it turned out to be too late for her? She tried not to think about that. After all, there was nothing she could do to prevent either outcome. She could simply ease the pain that came before.

"Did you and Mama get some good bonding in?" her father asked, watching her from the door frame.

"It's hard not to root for her," Abigail admitted. "But I still don't think we should keep them long term."

"Banish the thought." He clucked his tongue and wagged a finger at her. "When God sends you a gift, you don't just send it back. These pups were meant to find our church, and that's where they belong."

"So now they're the church's pets?" she said flatly.

It seemed her father's plans for these dogs were growing by the minute. Before the end of the night he'd have them signed up to compete for blue ribbons at the Westminster Kennel Club.

He chuckled as if privy to her private speculations. "Not pets. I was thinking more like working dogs."

Abigail forced down a giggle of her own. It would have cost her too much to let laughter in twice that day. "Working dogs? But they're so small! What are they going to do? Pull a sled the next time it snows?"

Her father's eyes glimmered, but he said nothing as he returned to the kitchen.

Abigail eased herself up from the floor and followed him. "What kind of work are they going to do for the church?"

"Whatever the Lord decides is good enough for me," he answered, plopping another steak into the frying pan.

"Wait. You're serious, aren't you?"

"As a heart attack" came the response.

"I always knew you were crazy, but this seems beyond your normal. You know all of Charleston will be talking about this before no time at all."

"Good, let them talk. Maybe then they'll come to church to see for themselves."

"More like they'll come to see the infamous Church Dogs of Charleston."

"Now, that does have a nice ring to it," he answered with yet another chuckle before turning and pushing a tea plate stacked with sliced steak into her hands. "Go see if you can get some food in that poor dog. After that, we'll work on you."

CHAPTER 4

ABIGAIL

Abigail could scarcely sleep that night. After her third time waking up in the wee hours, she officially gave up and went to hold vigil over the Chihuahuas.

Once in the living room, she found a plate of sugar cookies and gingerbread men waiting beside a glass of milk. Had her father put these out for tradition's sake, or did he have a feeling she'd rouse early and need a snack?

Why they were there didn't much matter, because food was one of the few joys Abigail still luxuriated in from time to time. She chose a gingerbread figure with chocolate icing hair and a red licorice smile, and bit into it with delight.

This one had to be her.

Growing up, she and her father had decorated dozens upon dozens of cookies each year, fashioning each to look like someone they knew from the church. She'd taken that tradition with her when she married Owen and moved into base housing. In fact, last year they'd had quite the laugh over her interpretation of his commanding officer.

This year, she'd skipped out on baking with her father. She'd skipped out on many things, not quite ready to attempt normality just yet. The baby inside her, she knew, presented a ticking clock. She'd need to be strong, healthy, and happy when he or she arrived. It wouldn't be fair to push her grief onto the child. After all, the poor thing would already be starting life one parent short.

Abigail took another bite of the warm cookie and glanced over to the basket of sleeping puppies nearby.

Mama Mary caught her eye, her little nose sniffing high in the air as if she needed two senses to confirm she had a visitor. And then, the tiny dog gently worked her way out of the basket and waddled over to Abigail.

"What is it, girl?" Abigail asked.

The dog cocked her head to one side, then slowly pulled herself into an upright position. Her two front paws clawed at the air in the most adorable bout of begging Abigail had ever witnessed in her whole life.

She smiled at the mother dog, glad to see she was already feeling so much better. "I'm not sure this is good for you, sweetie," she explained, frowning at the frosting smeared across her fingers even after the cookie had disappeared into her mouth. "Actually, they're not very good for me, either. Let's see if we can find something better in the kitchen."

Together, the mom and mom-to-be trotted into the kitchen and peeked into the fridge. It was flowing with abundance even more than usual. It seemed that this time of year every little old lady in her father's congregation wanted to help feed the poor single pastor—especially this year since he now came with a tragic widowed daughter and a yet-to-be-born grandchild.

Abigail selected a chicken and rice casserole from amongst the bounty and pulled it from the fridge. "We really need to pick you up some proper dog food as soon as the stores open again," she said, dishing out a serving for each of them. She stuck her plate in the microwave and put Mama Mary's on the tiled floor.

The dog sniffed it and sat without taking even the tiniest of bites. She glared at Abigail as if trying to tell her something. Just what that was, Abigail hadn't the faintest idea.

"Sorry, I don't speak dog," she said, grabbing her plate from the microwave before it could beep and disturb the still sleeping members of their household—especially the puppies. Their mother deserved whatever little bit of break she could get, especially if it meant getting more meat on her fragile bones.

Abigail carried her plate over to her favorite chair, surprised when Mama Mary chose to follow her out to the living room and continue her begging there.

"I just gave you some," Abigail reminded her, gesturing toward the kitchen where the other helping of fine Southern comfort food sat untouched.

For some reason unbeknownst to Abigail, these words encouraged the dog who attempted to jump up on the chair with her. However, she couldn't quite make the whole leap and fell back down to the floor.

"What?" Abigail laughed despite herself. "Do you want mine?"

The little dog glanced from Abigail's face to her plate and back again, causing her to laugh even harder. This time she didn't even scold herself for the happy gesture. Well, at least not much.

"Okay, have it your way," she said, offering the

plate to the hungry Chihuahua who immediately dug in and made fast work of cleaning the plate.

Abigail was just about to return to the kitchen to warm a second plate for herself when her father appeared at the end of the hallway, rubbing sleep from his eyes. "Morning already?" he asked with a giant overhead stretch.

"Not exactly," Abigail admitted, feeling a bit more reserved now that another human was around. Somehow it was easier to let her cruel inner dialogue rest in Mary's presence. Maybe because, inexplicably, it felt as if the dog understood in a way even Abigail's father couldn't—in a way she had yet to figure out for herself, too.

"Us girls were just having a late night snack," she added, continuing to the kitchen and thrusting open the fridge. "Want some?"

"Oh, what are we having? Actually, you know what? It doesn't matter. I'll have two, please."

That was her father, though. If it was worth doing, then it was worth overdoing, which was exactly why they now had five new dogs to take care of. It was also why his pants had become increasingly snug around the middle after she'd left to make a new home with her husband.

Well, she was back now, and if she couldn't

straighten out her own life, maybe she could at least do some good in her father's.

She smiled coyly to herself as she served him a single portion.

It was for his own good, after all.

CHAPTER 5

PASTOR ADAM

I knew my daughter and that mama dog would be thick as thieves in no time at all. Only "no time at all" happened faster than even I'd dared to hope. By the time I woke up the next morning, I found Abigail smiling and laughing just like she used to in a time not so long ago.

What I'd give to have that time and that happy, hopeful version of Abigail back for good.

Of course, I still remember clear as a bell when I first heard the news of my poor son-in-law's departure. Abigail had been crying so hard I could scarcely understand the words as she spoke them. Somehow I knew before she even had to confirm the tragic passing. I knew my daughter inside out, but nothing I could have done would have prepared her for this untimely loss.

Regardless of all that, I still question myself to this day. If I'd worked harder to keep Abigail's mama around, would she have an easier time dealing with the loss of her husband?

These questions remained impossible to answer, but that didn't mean I'd ever stop asking them. Just that night, for example, I had lain awake in bed, thinking, praying, wishing, wondering if my baby girl would ever come back to me. The Lord works in mysterious ways, but sometimes it's quite difficult to see His plan when you're standing right in the middle of it.

Abigail herself seemed to have decided that there was no plan, or if there was, then it meant His only aim was to torment her in this life and quite possibly also the next. Even though I understood her need to question, it still broke my heart to watch her shut God out—and, in turn, to shut me out, too.

You have to understand, it wasn't so long ago that my wife, Rachael, abandoned the both of us—only, unlike Owen, she chose to do it. I know Abigail's husband would have given anything to stay with her and guide their child through life.

Even still, I sometimes wonder what Rachael is

doing with her life these days, but I also know not to pick at that particular wound. It's why I haven't succumbed to the allure of Facebook even though so many of my congregants do sorely wish I'd start an account there. The best way to avoid temptation is to *avoid temptation*, if you know what I mean.

Whether I should have talked with Abigail more about her mother, I still don't know. But what could it help now? In my heart and by the eyes of God, I'm still married to Rachael, even though she chose to walk away from our life together and has never once looked back.

Had I been a bad husband to her?

Was I a bad father to Abigail?

Whatever the answers might be, the only thing I want now is for my daughter to smile again. Well, that, and to find her way back into the Lord's waiting arms. I pray for her many times each day. It's like breathing—a sacred routine I need in order to keep on keeping on.

That's why when He sent those dogs I knew for a fact that my prayers were well on their way to being answered, and then… this morning, I saw the beginnings of that answer take shape. God is good!

CHAPTER 6

ABIGAIL

Abigail fell asleep in her favorite wingback chair sometime between three and four a.m. When she finally awoke to start the day, the room was brightly lit by the morning sun and her father had returned to the kitchen to make his famous Sunday morning fry-up.

Never mind that today was Friday.

And Christmas.

She padded over to the kitchen and gave her father a kiss on the cheek.

"Merry Christmas," he said, wrapping his arm around her in a tight, warm hug.

She returned his holiday wishes and asked, "What do you have planned for today? I'm sure the church is keeping you on a very busy schedule as always."

He grinned and shook his head. "Not this time. Today I have the full day free to celebrate with you and our five new family members."

Abigail scrunched up her nose in confusion until she realized… the dogs, he meant the dogs. "Well, don't back out of any plans on my account. I'll be fine on my own."

He clucked his tongue and dismissed her hesitation with that same self-assured smile he always offered when she had no choice in a matter. "That's what you say every day," he pointed out. "But *today* is Christmas. And I'm not taking no for an answer."

Abigail brushed a loose strand of hair behind her ear. She probably looked a fright. "Okay, but what's the question?" she teased.

"No question. Just you, me, and the dogs celebrating His birth and eating lots of good food. Now while I finish up in here, why don't you go check the stockings?"

Abigail smiled at the memory of so many years before. She and her father had a veritable treasure trove of holiday traditions, and unpacking her stocking was one of her most favorite.

"There's one for the little squirt, too!" her father called after her as she traced her way to the fireplace.

Reflexively, she brought a hand to her belly. Next

year she'd have an actual, real live baby with her—a small piece of Owen who would need her to show him the world and all its wonders.

That meant she had less than a year left to rediscover them for herself. No pressure. Nope. None at all.

She gently unhooked both stockings from the mantle place and sat cross-legged on the floor to inspect their contents.

Mama Mary sidled up to her, tail wagging furiously as her four puppies whimpered and searched the bed for their missing mother.

"I bet it's exhausting," Abigail confided in her. "Having four! I can barely picture having one. I don't think I'm ready."

The little brown and white dog came closer and pushed her head under Abigail's palm.

Abigail smiled and petted the dog as requested. This tiny little thing had braved incredible obstacles to keep her babies safe. Would Abigail know to do the same once her child was in this world? Would she simply snap out of it and do what was needed?

She wished she could know for sure. Maybe then she wouldn't worry quite so much. For now, though, she had a stocking to unpack.

"C'mere," she called to the Chihuahua, patting

her lap and waiting for the eager dog to climb up into it. "We'll open them together."

She started with her own, a handsome green velvet stocking with her name written across the top in red glitter. She'd had the same one since grade school. Truly, some things never did change, while others...

"Okay," she told the dog, then sucked in a deep breath to steady herself and reach her hand inside. The first thing she found was a stick of peppermint lip balm. After that, a white chocolate bar—her favorite.

She continued to extract item after item from the stocking. Most were pretty run-of-the-mill Christmas things: ornaments, costume jewelry, treats. But at the very bottom she found something quite different. A little book was wedged into the giant stocking's toe.

Even before she'd pulled it out, she knew what it was. The gold-gilded pages and tiny engraved letters on the cover confirmed it.

Her father had returned her very first Bible to her.

"Why did you give this to me?" Abigail demanded of her father when he came to join her in the living room, handing her a plate overflowing with all her favorite breakfast foods.

"It's tradition."

"Not the stocking. *This*." She held the little Bible up for him to see—as if he could forget.

Mary skittered off her lap and returned to her puppies.

"What? *The Bible?* It's not a dirty word, you know. You can say it."

"Fine. Why did you give me the *Bible*? You know how I feel about this stuff now."

"This stuff, huh?" He shook his head and took a seat beside her on the floor. "I know you're in a sad place right now, which is why I thought you might want to be reminded of happier times so that you could see that maybe life isn't all bad."

"Happier times like when my mother abandoned me?" she asked, tucking the little book back into her stocking—out of sight, out of mind—before taking a deep, shuddering breath. Most days she tried not to spare a single thought for her selfish runaway mom, especially on the holidays. She hadn't earned the right to be a part of their world. Not anymore.

"We had a good life together, you and me," her father said with a sigh of his own. "We still do."

Abigail brought her knees up to her chest and hugged them tight. She didn't have the strength for this—not now, not ever. "I'm sorry, Dad. I don't mean to take this out on you. It's kind of why I wanted to be alone today."

"And it's exactly why I wouldn't leave you to your own devices." He lowered himself to the floor beside her, sitting close but not reaching out to touch her. "Wallowing solves nothing, baby girl. Owen wouldn't want you to live this way."

"It's only been a few months," Abigail sputtered, unable to look at him. "At least give me time to deal with my grief."

"Take all the time you need. I just want to make sure you know you're not alone. You've got me, and you've got God."

When Abigail continued to stare stonily at her feet, he added, "The dogs, too. They're here for you, and I'm willing to bet you need them just as much as they need you."

CHAPTER 7
ABIGAIL

They spent the rest of Christmas day watching their favorite holiday movies and keeping a close eye on Mama Mary and her puppies. By the end of it, Abigail was glad her father hadn't left her alone, but she also felt exhausted from the lack of sleep the night before coupled with all the time spent being social today—even if it was just with her dad.

"I'm going to hit the hay," she announced, hugging him goodnight. "Thank you for today."

As she padded to her room, she heard the scratch of little toenails following close behind. Sure enough, she turned to see the mother Chihuahua standing right at her heels.

"Good night, Mama Mary," she cooed. "See you in the morning."

But when she began walking again, the dog continued on after her.

"Hey, what are you doing? Go back to your puppies," Abigail urged her.

But Mama Mary just plopped her butt down and beat her twitching tail against the wood floor.

"Well, will you look at that! Looks like she needs you just as much as those puppies need her," her father said, rising from his chair with a chuckle. "Let's get them settled in your room."

"Why do you like me so much?" Abigail asked the Chihuahua, who merely tilted her head and widened her dark eyes in response.

Her father continued to laugh as he squeezed past with the makeshift bed of puppies. "Well, why wouldn't she? I mean, what's not to love?"

Oh, everything, Abigail wanted to respond, but bit her tongue. She'd once liked the person she was, but lately she didn't even recognize what she'd become. Could a few months really change a person so completely? And, even more worryingly, would she ever find her way back?

At least taking care of Mary and her litter of wee ones would provide a bit of a distraction to the unending monotony that filled her days lately. But she worried about allowing herself to become too attached. What if the dogs were also ripped away like a bloody bandage? What if she lost them the way she had lost Owen?

It hurt to open herself back up, even if it was just to a scraggly little dog. And yet, how could she say no when the brave mother Chihuahua clearly craved her friendship?

"You can stay with me tonight," she told the dog at last. "But tomorrow we're going to find your owners. They must be worried sick."

Her father sent her a knowing glance. "Since you're planning to go out, would you also get dog food, a new bed, a crate, collars, leashes… basically the works?"

Abigail sighed and paused in the doorway to her bedroom. "What? No, I'm not going out. I thought I could start an Internet search. I'd be happy to order whatever supplies you need from Amazon, but don't you think you're jumping the gun just a bit here?"

"What I think," he said, studying his daughter with a tender expression now, "is that you haven't left the house for weeks. This will be good for you. Besides, it's high time."

"But you said to take as long as I need to," she

reminded him. Of course, she wanted to get better, but that was much easier said than done. Being around other people—people who recognized her as the good pastor's daughter, no less—would only make things harder.

"Getting on with life doesn't mean you're letting go of Owen," he said, eyeing her cautiously.

He knows he's pushing me. He's doing it on purpose! she realized, though she was completely unsurprised by this revelation. After all, it was her father's way. If there was some poor soul in need of fixing, he was always first in line to volunteer for the job.

Her father shrugged as if that were enough to downplay his meddling. "All you need to do is go to the pet store, get what we need, then come right back. I'm way behind on prepping my sermon for Sunday. You'd be doing me a big favor. Mama Mary, too."

Abigail knew she would eventually have to stop hiding, but it still felt too soon to face the pitiful glances and repetitive platitudes of the various people about town. Grief wasn't a team sport, and she had no extra energy to help others deal with Owen's death. She hardly had enough to keep herself going.

Even if it was just a quick little trip to the pet store, she knew it would take a lot out of her. She also knew if she didn't go, her father would continue to pick at her until she finally caved. When it came right down to it, she might as well get it out of the way now.

"Okay," she conceded at last, bringing forth a big grin from her father. Even Mama Mary seemed to smile as she returned to nursing her puppies and watched the conversation unfold from her new spot in Abigail's room.

"But," she added, "if I do this, you can't force me to leave the house again for at least another week." She wasn't going to give in unless she could get a little out of this agreement, too.

"If that's what it takes," her father said, continuing down the hall without another word. Something told her he was already plotting how to break the deal they'd only just made.

He sure was lucky she loved him so much!

CHAPTER 8

ABIGAIL

The next morning, Abigail slid into her favorite pair of sweatpants, threw her hair in a messy bun, and headed to the pet store as soon as it opened. She normally didn't like big chain establishments, but the idea of being one of many anonymous shoppers in pet supply super stores around the country appealed to her that day.

Her waistband cut into her stomach as she sunk down into the driver's seat of her poor neglected vehicle. Soon she'd be able to feel the baby kick, and shortly after that, others would notice the growing bump at her midsection. She zipped up her loose hoodie, hoping it would be enough to hide her tummy from gossiping onlookers, then put the car in drive.

Having been born and bred in Charleston, she hadn't had much opportunity to drive through snow. Luckily, last night's blizzard had mostly melted into slush. Add to that the fact few cars were out on the road so early on the day after Christmas and she could handle it just fine. With any luck, she could get in and out of the store without running into anyone she knew, then within half an hour she'd be able to put this whole miserable errand behind her.

Abigail thanked her lucky stars when she noticed only one other vehicle in the enormous parking lot. She could do this. She could buy dog food without incident or embarrassment. Because if she couldn't, there would truly be no hope left for her.

First the dog food, then the world.

It felt silly putting so much importance on a simple errand, but it was the first normal thing she'd done since receiving news of Owen's death all those weeks ago. She grabbed a buggy from the carousel out front and pushed it into the overly bright store with the wind blowing at her back, urging her forward.

Right, dog food.

She'd never had a dog before so wasn't sure what the best brand was and didn't feel like pulling out her phone and researching in the middle of the aisle. With no other options left, she grabbed a bag that sported a dog who looked like Mama Mary on the front. She also grabbed a few cans of wet food that apparently tasted like filet mignon—*well, la-dee-dah*—before continuing to the next aisle.

Less than ten minutes later, her buggy was bursting with an assortment of toys, treats, and comfort items, all for Mama Mary and her puppies.

Which reminded her she'd forgotten to print out the flyer she'd designed to help locate the mother dog's owner. She'd wanted to give it to the cashier and request that she share it with anyone who stopped by, but it was too late for that now—and she definitely wasn't leaving the house again if she could avoid it.

So back to Plan A, then.

She'd start a social media campaign with the goal of reuniting Mary with her real owners. Back before she became a hometown hermit, she'd boasted a thriving freelance graphic design business. Perhaps those skills could help attract the right eyes in this scenario, too, and could help find Mary's owner quicker. After all, a picture said a thousand words—and a pretty picture got the point across that much better.

She smiled to herself. It was decided then, and she was almost home free. With a sharp turn of her shopping buggy, she headed toward the checkout lane, hoping she had everything her father had requested and that she had a large enough wad of bills in her pocket to cover the expense.

"Excuse me, Miss?" a husky voice called from behind her.

Abigail froze. She knew that voice, or at least a younger version of it. But she wasn't supposed to see anyone she knew here. She was supposed to be an anonymous shopper. She—

"Um, you dropped this." He wheeled his buggy next to hers and handed her a stuffed dinosaur toy.

Why, of all the rotten luck... It took all Abigail's Southern gentility to avoid cursing a string of not-so-nice words at the top of her lungs right there in the middle of the mega mart.

"Wait, Abigail Elliott? Is that you?" His chocolate eyes widened and his voice grew light, happy. "Well, fancy running into you here."

She hesitated before offering an uncomfortable smile and saying, "Hi, Gavin."

Yes, that same Gavin who'd escorted her to the freshman dance, the same Gavin who had once made her heart beat with wild abandon...

He was the same Gavin, but she wasn't the same Abigail.

CHAPTER 9

ABIGAIL

Abigail's heart pounded like an unwelcome visitor inside her chest. She'd worried about running into one of the little old ladies from her father's church, but never would she have guessed she'd be standing in the middle of an empty store the day after Christmas making small talk with her eighth grade crush turned ninth grade boyfriend.

Just the mere mention of Gavin Holbrook had once sent a swoony sigh rumbling right through her. Now, it set off a sigh of a different kind all together.

Oblivious to her torment, Gavin's smile widened to show off a row of perfectly straight teeth. Apparently all those years of braces had done him right. "I haven't seen you in forever," he whispered as if she were a thing to be worshipped rather than avoided.

Before Abigail could hesitate, he'd wrapped both arms around her in a tight hug. Of course, this sent her heart galloping even quicker. She glanced past his shoulder and into his buggy where an enormous tub of cat litter sat beside a bag of cat kibble and a baggie of cat nip.

"It's okay. I'm fine," she said, trying to remember if Gavin had owned a pet feline growing up or if he'd only recently become a cat person.

"Well, of course you're fine," he answered, pulling back to study her at hardly an arm's length. How she wished he would move on, or at least move back. "The years have been more than fine to you. You look great!"

She shook her head and slipped out of his hug with as much grace as she could muster given the situation. It was strange that he hadn't apologized for her loss yet. Most people did that the moment they laid eyes on her. Still, any minute now, he'd remember the news about Abigail's husband and pull into full-on pity mode.

"You must be back for the holidays, right? How much longer are you here? Can I take you out to dinner?" He paused to flash another mega-watt smile her way before concluding with, "You know, for old time's sake?"

She watched in slow motion as Gavin's gaze fell toward her hand and the small but sparkling diamond she still wore every day to honor her vow to Owen.

"Oh," he said. "I didn't realize… I mean, let's go out as just friends. Because we are, right? Friends?"

She frowned, feeling mortified for Gavin. How could he not know? "Didn't you hear about…?" Abigail let her voice trail off.

"That you got married? I guess I hadn't. A belated congratulations." He smiled again, a lesser smile this time.

"No." She twisted her hands together. While she'd dreaded everyone knowing, it was somehow worse that Gavin hadn't heard—that she'd need to be the one to tell him.

"I mean I was married, but…" She paused and risked a glance up at him, who watched her with wide eyes. He really didn't know. "Um, he died."

Gavin cursed under his breath. "I had no idea. I'm so sorry, Abigail."

"And I'm pregnant," she added without hesitation, hoping that this reveal would curtail any lingering attraction he may harbor for her.

"With your…? I don't know how to say this

right." Gavin turned red as he struggled to find the appropriate words. "With your husband's baby?"

She nodded. This was the end now. He'd make an excuse and run off. They always did. Nobody knew how to handle Abigail these days. Only her father even still tried.

Gavin's expression grew tender as if he could reach right in and feel the pain in her heart. "So it's a really recent loss then?"

Abigail nodded and choked back a sob. She wasn't sure how she'd expected him to respond, but it certainly wasn't with the tender hug that followed. That made two hugs in the space of five minutes, she noted.

Gavin held her as she cried right there in the middle of the pet emporium. Luckily, no one else was there to see save a few stray workers who gave them a wide berth.

"Well, now I'm definitely not taking no for an answer," he said with a smile as the two of them pulled apart. "When are we having dinner?"

"Dinner? No, I can't. I'm not ready to date. I'm not sure I'll ever be."

He shook his head. "No, not a date. As friends, like I said before. It seems like you could use a friend now more than ever."

"But..." She couldn't think of an argument to offer, but she also had no reason to say yes. It was so much easier to hide out alone in her father's house, especially now that she had the company of the Chihuahuas and a personal mission to find Mama Mary's owner.

"I promise no funny business," Gavin said, which is the same thing he'd told her father when arriving to pick her up for freshman year homecoming.

The déjà vu made Abigail titter softly, just like she would have back in high school when chatting with a cute boy, a boy like Gavin.

Gavin grabbed hold of this opportunity and refused to let go. "So you do remember what fun we used to have? Remember how we used to stay up and talk on the phone past midnight?"

She nodded and twisted her hands on the bar of her buggy, eager to make her escape.

"We could do that again," he pressed. "I'll catch you up on my life, and you catch me up on yours. Or don't. Look, I don't know the protocol for this. I don't want to pressure you, but it really does seem like you could use someone in your corner."

She sniffed and tried to smile. When that didn't work, she said, "You mean because I'm crying in the middle of the pet store on the day after Christmas?"

He shrugged before offering her another wholehearted grin. "Well, that, and I've gotta believe we ran into each other like this for a reason. We're the only two people in all of Charleston up and about right now, almost like it's fate."

"I don't believe in fate," Abigail answered quickly.

"But you could use a friend," he pointed out.

Oh, he was persistent.

She liked that in a way, but did Abigail really want a friend? She found it tiring enough to hang out with her father, and she loved him more than anyone else left in this world. Then again, what could one dinner hurt? Now that he knew her situation, there was no way he'd put the moves on her, and he always had been a good listener…

Okay, then. It was decided.

"Do you like puppies?" she asked with a guarded smile.

CHAPTER 10

PASTOR ADAM

Well, imagine my surprise when Abigail returned home with company. I recognized that school boy Gavin right away, and from the awkward expression plastered clear across his face, it seemed he remembered me, too.

Had it really been fifteen years since I'd reminded him to treat my daughter as the lady she is, else he'd be meeting the business end of my shotgun?

True, I didn't have a shotgun then—still don't—but he didn't know that. And it seemed my words had stuck with him over the years, too. He hauled in all the heaviest bags and supplies while Abigail moseyed in with a mostly empty shopping bag that held soft toys for when the puppies were old enough to begin using their choppers.

They still hadn't opened their eyes, and from the talking to I'd had with Mr. Manganiello just a short bit ago, it seemed they wouldn't for at least another week. I smiled just thinking where the pups would be in seven days' time—and, more importantly, where my daughter might be with them. Especially if it only took one small trip out of the house for her to make —or in this case, remake—a friend all on her own.

"Mr. Elliott," the all grown-up version of little Gavin said with a curt nod in my direction.

"I prefer Pastor Adam," I told him, trying to recall when exactly was the last time I'd seen him in church on any given Sunday.

"Oh, right," he said with a laugh. "I forgot since… Well, my folks moved us to the Chapel Assembly when I started dating Abigail. Said my mind needed to be on God—and not girls."

"Good of them," I answered with a chuckle. Seems his parents had their priorities straight, and I hoped he did, too. Especially if he planned to spend any significant amount of time with my Abigail. Come to think of it, I couldn't even remember why he and my daughter had called their young love quits all those years ago. Hopefully that meant it wasn't too gruesome.

"I got the things you asked for," Abigail said, shooting me a warning look. But warning me of what? I honestly hadn't the faintest.

"Gavin wanted to see the puppies," she explained, leading the friend turned stranger turned back into friend again to her bedroom.

I cleared my throat, ready to protest, but my daughter turned back toward me with such vim and vigor in her eyes that I swallowed my words back down. Instead, I followed along more of a force of habit than a lack of trust in my girl. Besides, I had too many questions about this new development in our day that I'd rather not leave her answering them to chance. I needed to find out why Gavin was here and what he wanted with Abigail whatever way I could.

"They're so tiny," he said, using the tip of his index finger to stroke each of our church dogs in turn. "They can't be more than a couple of days old."

"Probably not," she agreed.

"Do you know anything about dogs?" I asked from where I stood, leaning against the door frame with my arms crossed over my chest.

"Afraid not," he said with a grimace. "I'm more of a cat person."

If I'd been born a Catholic, I would have crossed myself in response to that one. Of course I loved all of God's creatures, but I'd always loved dogs just a little bit extra. We hadn't had them while Abigail was growing up because her mother Rachael had been allergic—and, well, a part of me always hoped she'd walk back into our lives and pick up where she left off.

"Be nice, Dad," Abigail warned again, a look of exasperation etched across her normally sorrowful face. At least exasperation was an improvement.

"I'm always nice," I answered, an idea popping into my mind as I watched the two young people coddle Mama Mary and her puppies. "It sure is nice to see you again, Dr. Holbrook."

"It's good to see you both, too," he answered with a brief, questioning glance my way. "Although I'm sorry about the circumstances."

This raised more questions than it answered. I'd called the man a doctor, hoping he would correct me and reveal his true profession—but he'd stayed blessedly silent.

"So, how is the medical business treating you these days?" I pressed further.

Abigail sighed, but Gavin answered me all the

same. "I hear it's good, but I'm not in that business myself, so couldn't say for sure."

"Daddy, could we please have some privacy?" Abigail asked, her exasperation had turned to outright frustration.

"Oh, yes. I'll just be on my way. Good to see you again," I said, knowing when I'd been defeated at my own game.

Still, Gavin and I exchanged nods, then I carried myself away, hoping I'd still be able to overhear any conversation from the living room.

CHAPTER 11
ABIGAIL

Abigail brought her hands to her cheeks to hide the sudden rush of heat. Her pale skin meant that she would often turn red at even the slightest provocation. If Gavin noticed her sudden shyness, he at least didn't say anything to further embarrass her. Her father had done enough of that already.

"Sorry about him," she whispered when she was certain the meddling pastor had moved out of earshot.

Gavin laughed, and his eyes crinkled at the corners just as they always had. She liked that some things didn't change, no matter how much life threw at you.

"I think it's sweet how concerned he is over you,"

he said after a pause. "And that he thought he was being so stealthy with all that Dr. Holbrook business."

He rolled his eyes, then turned his attention back to the puppies. "I think this one's my favorite," he said, gently petting a mostly black puppy with a little white line running down the top of her head all the way to her impossibly tiny nose.

"How can you have a favorite?" she asked, grabbing tight to the topic change and running with it. "They all act the same."

"Nah, you can already see their personalities coming through. See how this one pushes its way in over the other puppies and makes sure it gets the best spot? He's a spunky little guy and will be a lot of fun when he's old enough to play."

"*She*," Abigail corrected. "That one's a girl."

Gavin drew his hand away from the puppy and turned to face Abigail. "Oops. I guess my lack of dog knowledge is showing. What's her name?"

"She doesn't have one yet. None of them do except for Mama Mary," she admitted, even though she'd definitely been tempted to preempt her father's waiting period and just name the puppies herself. "Dad says he's going to let the Sunday School kids pick names."

"Oh, boy. That probably means they'll all be named after princesses and superheroes then." Gavin leaned in toward the puppies again and gave the mother dog a scratch between her ears.

"Well, there are worse ways to name a dog, I suppose." Abigail thought of the little one growing inside her belly. She didn't have any names picked out for him or her yet, either. Nothing felt right in a world where her child would be born half an orphan. She guessed if it were a boy she could name him for Owen, but what if she had a girl? She had no idea which she preferred or whether she would love her child on sight as all good mothers were supposed to do. None of it felt real yet even though the clock continued to tick away without missing a single second.

"What's wrong?" Gavin asked, his brow crumpled with concern.

"Nothing," she answered reflexively and swiped at dry, itchy eyes. "Well, actually everything, but that's not your fault."

Gavin cleared his throat, then waited for her to look up at him before he spoke. "I hate seeing you like this. You were always this bright beam of sunshine growing up." His smile faltered before returning full blast. "Actually, I think I had a crush on you ever since the first day I met you on the swings in Kindergarten. Remember that?"

"No," Abigail answered with a shake of her head. "I'm sorry. I really don't."

He placed his hand on hers and gave it a quick squeeze before letting go. "When we were finally placed in the same class in second grade, I insisted the teacher sit me right behind you."

Now this she couldn't believe. Gavin hadn't said a single kind word to her until middle school at the absolute earliest. "But you were awful to me in second grade!" she argued. "I went home crying more than once."

"Yeah, little boys aren't the best at romance." He chuckled, drawing a soft giggle from her as well. "But I finally got it right in eighth grade when I asked you to the end-of-year dance and even braved your father to come pick you up."

"That was a good night," Abigail said with a wistful sigh. She could still remember almost every minute of that special day. "I remember thinking the gymnasium looked absolutely magical."

"Yeah, a great night followed by a great year. But then stupid teenager stuff got in the way and we broke up. I never stopped caring about you, though, you know. Junior year I tried to rack up the courage to ask you to prom, but then Pippa Jackson asked me first and I figured I might as well go with her rather than risk you saying *no*."

"I would've said *yes*," Abigail realized with a start. "I ended up staying home because all of my friends had dates except for me."

"Unbelievable," Gavin teased with a roll of his eyes. "Seems we had a few different near misses in our day, but still, here we are again. Together."

She sighed and wondered what more she could say to convince Gavin she wasn't ready for a relationship—not now and possibly not ever again.

"As friends," he added before she had to correct him. "I know you're hurting and I want to help. I care about you, Abigail, and besides, I'm not looking for a relationship either."

She raised an eyebrow in his direction. "Oh? Is that so?"

"Work keeps me busy. Your father was half right, by the way. I actually am a doctor, but for teeth." He flashed his pearly whites at her as if they alone offered the proof she needed.

She scrunched up her face at that reveal. "You grew up to be a dentist?" She'd never pictured Gavin as a dentist. Truth be told, she couldn't really picture him as anything rather than the boy she knew in high school.

"Nah, an endodontist. We're way better than your run-of-the-mill dentists."

She knew that word, and it wasn't a good one. Owen had been severe pain before finally visiting the base-recommended endodontist for an emergency root canal. And now Gavin was saying this was what he had voluntarily chosen to do for a living? Too bizarre.

"Aren't you the guys who give people root canals?" she asked, trying her best to keep a straight face. This felt just like the old days when they'd tease each other about who got the higher score on a test or who could skip a rock further across the beach. "Hate to break it to you, but nobody likes a root canal."

But Gavin was clearly a man who loved what he did and was ready to defend it. "See, that's where you're wrong," he argued. "Everyone talks about how bad they are, but it's really the pain leading up to them that's bad. Actually, root canals end that pain, and that makes me a professional pain ender."

Abigail studied him for a moment, noting how his blond hair hung shaggy over his forehead and how he'd grown into the long arms and legs he'd sported as a teen. He seemed sincere and without a hidden agenda. It didn't make any sense, but then again, they'd both grown up so much in the years since high school. Gavin had become a doctor, for goodness' sake. She needed to give him a chance. At the very least his company offered less pressure than her father's. Maybe it wouldn't be the worst thing in the world to have a friend she could confide in.

"So you want to end my pain?" she asked after taking a dry gulp.

"Yes, ma'am." Always the good Southern boy. Always sincere, a gentleman. He hadn't changed one bit other than this crazy new job of his.

She watched as his eyes lit with mischief.

"I'm not too sure a root canal would help here," Gavin said with a shrug. "But we can always try it just in case."

Abigail laughed softly and bumped her shoulder into his as the puppies continued to scrabble for the best nursing spot.

Yes, it felt nice to have a friend.

CHAPTER 12

ABIGAIL

Abigail watched as her father did up his tie in front of the old antique mirror that hung in their foyer.

"Are you sure you won't come this morning?" he asked, making eye contact with her reflection and offering a wheedling smile.

She pretended to think it over, already knowing full well what her answer would be. *"Hmm.* Didn't you promise not to ask me to leave the house again for at least a week after the whole thing yesterday?"

He shrugged and patted his tie flat after finishing the knot. "I thought maybe things had changed since you invited that Gavin fella over. And besides, the kids will be naming the puppies today. Don't you want to be a part of that?"

"No, I haven't changed my mind, and, no, I don't need to be there. The puppies are too little to go anyway. Take the pictures I gave you to help inspire the kids, and I'll stay here to watch after the dogs in person."

Her father turned abruptly and placed a hand on her shoulder, regarding her with a frown that told her exactly what was coming. They had the same conversation every Sunday since she'd moved back home.

"One of these days you're going to have to make peace with God," he said softly.

"Maybe, but today's not that day."

He looked like he wanted to say more but swallowed back whatever it was and cleared his throat, then gave her a kiss on the cheek instead.

Abigail watched him go, then waited until she heard her father's car start up in the drive before finally letting out a long, shaky breath. Today was the day she planned to find Mama Mary's owners. Even though only a few days had passed since her father brought the Chihuahuas home from his Christmas Eve sermon, she already felt herself getting attached— and that was a huge problem.

It would be just her luck for the cuddly creatures to get ripped away by their rightful owners just as Abigail had finally allowed herself to fall in love with them. She needed to find them sooner than later, even if her dad and all the Sunday school kids would be sorely disappointed at the loss of their "church dogs." After all, the longer they waited, the harder it would be on everyone.

She'd already taken photos of the mother dog from multiple angles and designed a handful of sharable social media graphics and printed flyers that she hoped her father might be willing to distribute around town to save her the trouble. Now she just needed to figure out where to post her notices online, and if all went according to plan, the dogs would be returned to their original owners by nightfall.

What kind of person loses a heavily pregnant dog in the middle of a snow storm? she wondered. And what if that bout of negligence wasn't just a one-time thing? What if Mama Mary often escaped or got lost on the streets? Would it really be best for the dogs—especially the tiny puppies—to go back to an owner like that?

She shook her head, hoping to dislodge the guilt that had set up shop inside her head. But the gesture didn't help. Nothing did. The guilt would probably stick with her no matter what she decided. After all, not trying to find the owners wasn't an option either. Why did this have to be so hard?

She fired up her laptop which—other than designing the graphics to aid in her search—had been badly neglected as of late. Once it had finished running a slew of updates, she logged into Facebook to begin posting her found dog campaign far and wide. A little red notification drew her eyes to the friend requests section where a smiling picture of Gavin greeted her.

She clicked accept and almost immediately received a private message: *Pffhew! For a while there I wasn't sure you were going to be my friend.*

Gavin's name blinked at her until she clicked the window to type out her response: *I'm not on much. Just logged in to see if I can find the dogs' owner.*

Need any help?

I'll let you know. Thanks.

She hated to be abrupt, but if she didn't focus now, she'd never find who Mama Mary belonged to. When it seemed like Gavin had nothing more to say, she minimized their chat and did a search for rescue groups in the area. She was able to join two straightaway, but the others all had a membership approval process, meaning she'd already reached a dead end for the time being.

Frustrating.

Before logging off and waiting for the dogs to

awake from their morning nap, she decided to check her newsfeed. Most of the updates were either from members of her father's church or her friends from back on base. It felt odd seeing them continue with their lives as if nothing had changed when everything in Abigail's world was different.

She quickly scrolled past anything that made her heart ache for Owen, finally stopping on a beautiful image of a fair-haired woman sitting in the snow with a gorgeous pair of huskies. *A FREE BOOK FOR THE ADVENTURER IN YOU* was written in huge block letters beside them.

Abigail clicked on the ad and was taken to a simple website with a place to enter her email and receive a free copy of the author's bestselling book based on her adventures with sled dog racing. Abigail doubted there was an "adventurer in her," as the ad claimed, but at the very least, this free book could help to pass time.

She entered her email and downloaded a copy to her computer.

Returning to Facebook, she spotted an ad for the local gynecological office asking her if she'd scheduled her yearly pap smear. It was creepy how much the social media site knew about her, and these very specific ads proved it. No, she hadn't scheduled a pap smear lately, which she suspected Facebook already knew, but she did need to find a new doctor for her prenatal care. Other than taking her vitamins and trying to eat somewhat healthy, she'd done very little to take care of her baby.

Part of her was terrified she'd burst into tears and not be able to stop crying when she came face to face with the baby on the big ultrasound screen—without Owen there to hold her hand and experience the moment with her. But she'd already waited too long as it was. She needed to be a good mother to her child, no matter how hard it was on her heart.

Abigail held one hand over her pulsing chest and used the other to click into the doctor's website. It was time to stop hiding from what needed to be done.

CHAPTER 13

ABIGAIL

Later that day, Abigail's father came home to tell her the children had named the puppies Brownie, Cookie, Cupcake, and Muffin—apparently, they had all been craving some rich desserts that morning. The names they'd picked were kind of cute, though, and surprisingly they did match the puppies quite well.

The white one with brown spots resembled a chocolate chip cookie. The mostly black puppy with a white stripe on its forehead could be a burnt brownie, she supposed, while the fawn colored dog reminded her of a banana nut muffin, leaving the one that most resembled its mother to be their Cupcake.

Ugh. It would be harder to give them up now that they had names. Of course, they might not have to ever say goodbye at the rate her search was going. She'd been approved to join a couple more groups and a few dozen people had reposted her pictures, but so far there were absolutely no leads.

She'd need to get the dogs into a vet soon. Maybe the staff there would have some ideas of where to search next. Heck, they might even recognize Mama Mary and know how to get in touch with her owner.

Abigail decided to make an appointment for the dogs once business hours started up again the next morning. Everything was slower because of the holidays, and that would continue for at least another week. She shuddered at the thought of ringing in a new year and thus ushering in her first full year as a widow. It would also be the year she welcomed her first—and probably only—child into the world.

There would be many more firsts on her own now that all her lasts with Owen were through. What a horrible epiphany!

The only lucky thing that happened all day was that the OBGYN's website allowed her to book her appointment directly online. Miraculously, they even had an opening for the following morning, which she nabbed right up. If her calculations were right, she'd be able to discover the baby's sex during her ultrasound tomorrow. This realization made her incredibly nervous. It would make everything that much more real, that much more imminent.

She chose not to mention the appointment to her father over dinner that night, knowing he'd insist on coming with her. Truth be told, she would rather face the doctor alone. After all, she'd need to get used to handling her parenting tasks solo—might as well start now.

She hardly caught a wink of sleep before waking up far too early the following morning. Mama Mary and her puppies continued to snuggle on the new fleece-lined dog bed she had purchased for them the day she'd run into Gavin who, by the way, hadn't messaged her again since she'd brushed him off the day before.

It was for the best. Thank goodness.

She'd already foolishly allowed herself to wonder what her life would be like now, if the two of them hadn't broken up back then, if she'd never fallen for Owen at all because she was still smitten with her high school sweetheart. This, of course, begged the question about whether it was better to have loved and lost…

Lately, she didn't think it was.

If she'd never met Owen, then she wouldn't be aching for him now. She wouldn't be facing a life alone as a single mother living with her pastor father in the same house she'd grown up in.

Of course, she felt terrible for thinking like that. It was almost like throwing away her memories of him altogether. If it had been the other way around, if she'd died instead of him, what would *his* life be like now? Well, *he* wouldn't be expecting a baby, for one. But would he mourn her or would he cry a little and move on?

Owen had always been the better person of the two of them, so no doubt he would choose the right response... whatever that was.

Abigail's phone buzzed on her dresser with an appointment reminder. Once again, she'd let giant snatches of time pass without doing anything more than wallowing in her own misery. She really needed to cut that out... if only she could figure out how.

Struggling up from the bed, she pulled on her favorite pair of jeans. When the button dug into her growing belly, she unsnapped them and used the same ponytail holder trick she'd used in college when that wretched freshman fifteen had settled over her hips. A quick loop around the button and a bit of a tug transformed her too-tight jeans into makeshift maternity wear.

This was the beginning.

She wouldn't be able to put off buying actual maternity clothes for too much longer, but maybe she could purchase them online and avoid having to go out to handle the dreaded task.

This made two outings in three days now, and she knew she'd need to help her father take the dogs into the vet that evening as well.

Just breathe. You've got this, she reminded herself.

After a quick splash of water on her face and a second ponytail holder to tie back her hair, Abigail took a series of deep breaths and headed out of the house.

Soon she would see her baby live on the big ultrasound screen. She'd even find out whether it would be a girl or a boy. That was a big deal, right? A huge deal!

So why wasn't she excited?

CHAPTER 14

ABIGAIL

Abigail held her breath as the ultrasound tech squeezed a line of cold gel onto her belly.

The tech hummed merrily as she slid the wand across Abigail's distended abdomen. "Do you want to know what you're having, or are we leaving it a secret until the big day?" she asked with the kind of smile that implied she absolutely loved her job.

"Sure," Abigail answered, trying to match the other woman's enthusiasm. This was her baby, after all. It was okay to get excited. It's what she was *supposed to* be feeling.

The tech continued to make occasional small talk as she took and retook various measurements. Luckily, she didn't ask about the father, a small miracle for which Abigail was extremely grateful. Instead, she said, "Your baby is measuring on the small side. Not small enough to be worried, but it explains why you're not showing much yet. Have you felt the baby kick?"

"Not yet," Abigail answered with a frown. Yes, a kick would definitely make her baby feel more real. So far she'd had a physically easy pregnancy and, for the most part, had kept her mind on Owen's loss rather than bonding with the child. "Should I have?"

"Many women do by now, but it's not uncommon for women undergoing their first pregnancy to feel the baby moving closer to twenty-six weeks. You're at about twenty. Maybe nineteen."

"What will it feel like? When the baby moves?" she asked, moving her eyes from the grainy image of her sleeping baby on the screen over to the other woman.

The tech gave a wistful smile as she continued to stare at the baby's heart thumping on the black and white monitor. "Every mother describes it a little differently. None of my girls were very rough and tumble on the inside or the out, so to me it felt something like bubbles popping or butterfly wings flapping."

"Girls," Abigail said, trying to feel something—

maybe hope, maybe dread, just *something*—at the thought of having a daughter of her own. "Am I having a girl, too?"

The tech's eyes widened and she dropped her voice conspiratorially. "Are you ready to find out?"

"Yes." Abigail held her breath as she waited for the tech to reposition her wand. Suddenly she desperately needed to know what she was up against. Maybe decorating a nursery and shopping for an infant wardrobe would help her finally move on past her grief and begin to feel excited that she wouldn't be the lone member of the Elliott-Sutton family any longer.

The tech snapped a picture of the screen and traced her cursor across the image to outline the baby's private bits. "Congrats, Mama. You're having a boy."

Abigail closed her eyes to keep in the tears that had begun to form. She still didn't know whether she felt happy about this news or saddened by it. The only thing she knew for sure is that she wished Owen were here to experience it with her. If she still believed in God, she could tell herself that her late husband was smiling down at her…

But she just couldn't.

"Do you know what you're going to name him?"

the tech asked, moving the wand in slippery circles as she searched for the next spot to measure.

"Yes," Abigail answered, surprising herself. This was one decision she didn't need to deliberate over at all. She knew exactly what her little boy was meant to be called.

"Owen," she whispered to the tech before saying it again louder, clearer. *Owen.*

Perhaps now the name would bring her joy. Perhaps now she could finally look forward instead of back.

"That's a nice name," the other woman said, not pressing for more. Somehow she just seemed to understand what Abigail needed from this exchange —and, even more importantly, what she didn't.

When Abigail and Owen had first started dating, she'd looked up the meaning of his name on a parenting website. Now they had come full circle, it seemed. Owen was a Welsh name, she remembered, meaning "desire born." But Abigail had never desired raising a child without his father. She had never desired becoming a widow in her twenties. Would new desires in life finally find her once this second Owen was born?

Owen, Jr. she thought, immediately deciding never to call her child that or the resulting nickname

—OJ. She would teach her son how to be a strong man, a good and honest one. And if she had a hard time doing that on her own, she knew her own father would always be there to support him, to support them.

And she couldn't think of a better man to serve as a role model for her son. After all, he had given up his whole world to make sure that hers had been magical growing up. Safe.

It wasn't his fault that life had thrown her such an unfair curve ball. But was it really God's, either? Her father had spent his entire life in pursuit of living a good life, of leading others to Jesus. He was the best man she knew. Could his beliefs really be fundamentally flawed?

…Or was it Abigail herself who was wrong? Damaged? Deeply flawed?

She looked again toward the monitor and watched as her son twisted into a new position, bringing his hands up to his mouth and eliciting a yelp of joy from the tech.

"Oh, look! Someone finally decided to join us. Hi, little guy," she said with a smile that matched the one that had stretched across Abigail's face, too.

"Hi, little Owen," she whispered, wiping away the beginnings of fresh tears. "I'm your mama."

CHAPTER 15

PATOR ADAM

I returned home from a morning meeting with the church elders to discover my only daughter had snuck off in my absence. Of course, almost immediately, I found myself wondering if she'd gone out with that Gavin fellow. And if that were the case, should I be grateful to him or suspicious of his motives?

Hmm, a tough question indeed.

A quick check on the puppies found all four content with full bellies. Mama Mary seemed to be well fed, too, so I left the five of them to whatever mid-day routine they'd established amongst themselves and continued my search of the rest of the house for my missing Abigail.

As I opened doors and flung back covers, I

attempted a little bit of math in my head. Mind you, math had never been my strong suit, but desperate times, desperate measures and such.

Okay, I told myself. *I found the puppies Thursday night. Abigail found Gavin Saturday morning. And now it was early Monday afternoon.* By last count, I was still up five dogs, up one questionable ex-boyfriend, and down one daughter.

Hmmm, indeed.

Maybe a few more calculations would help me sort this out.

Numbers, numbers… Owen's funeral had been about *three* months ago, which meant Abigail's baby was about *five* months along. Meanwhile my wife had been missing approximately *eighteen* years and seven months, give or take a week.

I had no idea where this left me now. I hadn't moved on relationally in close to two decades, but I had kept my head up and kept going on as if life were normal for my daughter's sake. Was she ready to do the same for her child?

Also, my wife was still—presumably—out there somewhere very much alive. We knew Owen's body rested peacefully six feet under while his soul enjoyed eternal paradise with His maker.

That made things different between Abigail and me.

But just how different, I found it difficult to quantify. If you divided my length of mourning by her length of mourning so far, carried the two, and multiplied by a factor of…

Nope, I surely had no idea how to solve for X when it came to this one. Or even what X represented, for that matter.

That was when my phone rang, zapping me straight out of my mathematical conundrum. The caller ID told me it was none other than my missing Abigail.

"Hello," I answered with a smile that almost made it hurt to talk. I'm not sure whether I was happier to have found Abigail's whereabouts or to be free of trying to calculate… whatever it was I had begun to calculate.

Her voice came out soft, so soft it was hard to hear over the thumping of my own heart.

"Speak up, dear," I shouted into the phone, trying to lead by example. "Are you okay?"

"I'm perfect," she said with that omnipresent sniffle of hers. *Perfect* was a word I hadn't heard her utter since the days before Owen's passing, which really made me wonder where she could be and why she was calling now. Luckily, I didn't have to ask.

She rushed straight into sharing her news, informing me, "I'm having a boy."

A boy. A boy!

I swear to you, more wonderful words have never been spoken, not before and not since. My baby girl was having a baby boy.

What really sent my heart spinning with happiness, though, was the pride in her voice as she made this announcement, the gratitude and love.

Soon Abigail would have a son, and I'd have my daughter back.

Plus, one very special grandchild to spoil rotten as only pappies, paw-paws, and gramps are welcome to do. I couldn't wait for my turn to come.

CHAPTER 16

ABIGAIL

A sudden burst of sadness overtook Abigail as the glass door to the doctor's office swung shut behind her. It was there in that tiny office she had felt the first flickers of excitement about becoming a mother, *there* she had truly committed herself to doing whatever it took to give little Owen the best life possible.

And that started with healing his mother.

Despite her newfound determination, she had no idea where to begin with such a lofty task. There was so much she needed to fix, so many parts of herself she needed to find again. The challenge seemed practically insurmountable.

But she simply had to find a way, no matter how long it took.

Head down, she hurried down the corridor that led back to the parking lot.

Maybe she could start with setting up the nursery. She'd been out of work for a while now, but she also had a modest sum remaining from big Owen's life insurance policy. If she was mostly frugal, with a few special splurge items here and there, she could craft something quite special for little Owen.

She just had to—

Oof!

"I'm so sorry," she sputtered into the stranger's chest. That's what she got for not watching where she was going. "I didn't mean to—"

Her voice fell away the moment she glanced up and spotted Dr. Gavin Holbrook smiling down at her with a bemused expression. "Fancy running into you here," he said with a smirk.

"You said that last time," she pointed out.

"And it's even truer this time. Where are you headed in such a hurry?"

"The baby store," she admitted. "I just found out I'm having a boy."

"Well, congratulations!" he said with not the slightest indication that he felt anything other than immense happiness for her. "I'd say this calls for a celebration. I was just about to take my lunch break.

Can you delay your shopping for—oh—I'd say an hour?"

She hesitated for a moment before remembering her resolution to be better for her baby. Friends were good and healthy. She needed this.

"Sure," she said with a smile as she reached into her purse for her keys. It got easier each time she forced a smile. Maybe soon she wouldn't have to fake it anymore. "But do you mind if I drive?"

Gavin sucked in a deep breath and leaned forward as if to reveal a secret. "*Uh oh*. Seems like someone still remembers what happened during driver's ed sophomore year."

She rolled her eyes at him. Some secret! "I'm pretty sure everyone in the tri-county area remembers. Who could forget some random guy driving straight into the school flagpole his first time out behind the wheel?"

"Hey! That wasn't some random guy. That was me!" He grabbed the lapels of his white lab coat and stood taller.

Abigail couldn't help but smirk at his ill-founded pride. "I'm not sure owning it makes the whole thing any better."

"Well, I assure you I'm a much better driver now."

He rooted in his pocket and pulled out a giant cluster of keys adorned with a pink fuzzy puff of a keychain.

She studied him for a moment before bursting out into her first whole laugh in what felt like ages. "As much confidence as all this inspires, I'd still rather not take any chances," she said when at last she had sobered enough to manage words.

"Have it your way." Gavin sighed and shoved his keys back into his pocket. "But if you're driving, I'm treating."

"If you insist," Abigail said as they wove through the parking lot and toward her old, beat-up sedan. She'd need to find something much safer before her baby arrived.

"Unbelievable," Gavin said, staring at her as if she'd sprouted a second head. "Is this the same car you had in high school?"

"Well, yes and no," she admitted, turning the key in the door because she hadn't bothered to replace the batteries in the automatic opener yet.

"It either is or it isn't. How can it be both?"

"Nice to know you live in a world without gray areas," she said, shooting a playful wink his way before sinking down into the driver's seat. It really did feel like old times with Gavin at her side, as if all the years since high school had melted away—all the problems, pain, and hurt.

"My car in high school was a '96 Saturn SL2," she explained after Gavin had joined her inside. "This is a '00."

"So you basically bought the same ancient car a second time?"

"Well, not exactly the same, but I couldn't find any '96s," she explained.

"But why?" he demanded. "This car is like twenty years old now. That's practically as old as we are!"

She shrugged, feeling scrutinized by his direct gaze. "Cars aren't super important to me. My first one always served me well, so when it was time to replace it I figured, why not get another just like it?"

Gavin stared slack-jawed at her, saying nothing.

"I guess maybe I'm a little bit sentimental," she admitted.

His eyes widened and his head jutted forward. "A little bit?"

"Okay, a lot. But so what? There are more important things in life than cars." She jabbed her key in the ignition and brought the engine to life, if for no other reason than to show Gavin that—yes—this dusty old car was reliable and—yes—it got her around just fine.

"You haven't changed at all," he said, appraising her with mirth in his eyes. "It's one of the things I always liked about you."

She turned away from him, wondering if it was too late to get out of this lunch. "What? How could you possibly say that? You only just found out about the car."

"Yeah, but not that you hang on to things that are important to you. Remember your room in high school? It had pink walls and unicorn decals. You still had all this white furniture with crystal knobs. It was the same set you—"

"Had in grade school," she finished for him. "I know." She risked a glance his way, unable to hide the embarrassed smile that burned its way onto her face. "It's still the same even now, you know."

"I figured it might be. The room you're sleeping in now with the puppies, though. It's not the same one you had back then."

"No," she said, looking over her shoulder before backing out of the parking spot at last.

"Why not? If you're so nostalgic, why keep your old room the same but not use it when you came back home?"

"My new room has my bedroom set from back at the base. With my husband." She set her mouth in a firm line, hoping he wouldn't ask any more questions for a while.

Gavin sank back in his chair and rubbed his hands on his pant legs. "You're a complex woman, Abigail Elliott."

"Abigail Elliott-Sutton," she corrected.

"It's like your two bedrooms, huh? You're hanging on to both."

She frowned. Why should she have to explain herself? So what if she cherished things a little more than was normal? Not everyone lost their husbands in their mid-twenties or their mothers in early grade school. She had to hang onto what mattered, because in some cases it was all she had left. But how could you explain that to someone who had never known loss?

"Relax," Gavin said, startling her as he placed a hand on her arm. The car swerved toward the curb in response. "I don't mean to give you a hard time. I like that things matter to you. It makes me think that maybe I mattered, too. Maybe I still matter." He paused before adding, "As a friend."

It was only then that Abigail realized he was absolutely right. Reviving her friendship with Gavin was the perfect way to rediscover who she'd been and bring back that happier, kinder person for her son.

She owed it to her baby, and she owed it to herself. Besides, it seemed Gavin was a little sentimental, too. He brought up the past even more than she did. "You do matter," she told him. "And I'm glad we're friends again."

CHAPTER 17

ABIGAIL

Abigail followed Gavin's directions as he navigated them through Charleston's Historic District straight to a locally famous restaurant called Poogan's Porch. If you were to ask her father, he'd claim that Poogan's was not quite as locally famous as their church's yearly nativity scene, but then again, he'd say the same thing about the Carolina Panthers as well.

"This doesn't seem like a quick lunch to me," she scolded her impromptu lunch date while eyeing the quaint yellow restaurant and its not so quaint double-decker box porch.

"I was in the mood for some Lowcountry cooking," he said, holding the door open for her so she could pass inside. "Besides, they get folks in and out quickly at lunch time. We'll be just fine."

Gavin pulled out a chair for Abigail, then pulled his keys from his pocket before taking a seat of his own. "We'll have two sweet teas and two orders of shrimp and grits," he told the hostess with a smile.

"Ordering for me, are you?" Abigail teased. Lucky for him, she liked just about everything. She also hadn't had shrimp and grits for a very long time, and everyone knew Poogan's Porch served them up best.

"Why order anything else when this one dish is perfection?" he asked with a sly smile. "I'm sure the others are perfectly delicious in their own right, but it doesn't seem I'll ever find out. As soon as I walk in that door, I know exactly what I want."

"And that's the shrimp and grits, huh?" She could think of far worse food addictions—far worse addictions, period. These days it felt almost as if she'd grown addicted to grief and solitude. Shrimp and grits would have been a much better choice.

"Precisely," he said, bringing her ribbing session to a close.

"Okay, so I have to ask. What's with the giant pink thing on your keys?" Abigail said, gesturing toward the giant heap of metal and fluff that sat beside his water glass.

"What, this old thing?" he asked with a laugh, picking up the bunch and handing it over to her. "A very special little lady gave me this pink poof and I haven't had the heart to take it off my keys, no matter how emasculating it might be."

Half a dozen questions raced through Abigail's mind. What child was so important to Gavin that he kept that silly thing proudly on display? Was he a father? A proud uncle? What wasn't he telling her, and would it be too nosy if she asked outright?

"You haven't told me much about you," she hedged. "Other than that you're a professional pain remover."

"Not much to tell," he responded with a shrug, casually dropping the keys into his lap and out of view, which didn't go unnoticed by Abigail.

"But you had a lot to say about your job."

"My job is my life these days. That and my Puss."

Abigail choked on her water. "Excuse me?"

He laughed at her expression of horror. "Puss in Boots, my cat. He's why I was at the pet store the other day. Why we found each other again."

She rapped her fingers on the table, resisting the urge to take another sip of water in case Gavin said something equally shocking once more. "You must know that's not a great name for a cat."

"Why not?" he chortled as his blue eyes danced with mischief. He clearly enjoyed making her squirm. "It was good enough for Antonio Banderas, it's good enough for me."

"*Um.*" Abigail leaned back as the waitress poured their drinks from a sweating pitcher of tea.

"Oh, c'mon. You know *Shrek!* The movie with the big green guy? Besides, it was fun to get a shock out of you," he teased. "Normally, I just call my cat 'Boots.' He's mostly brown tabby, but he's got these little white socks on his feet that are quite distinctive."

"So why not name him Socks?" she asked flatly, praying her cheeks hadn't turned as red as the lobster being served up two tables over.

He shook his head. "Nah, everyone names cats like him Socks. I had to be at least a little different."

"Gavin Holbrook," Abigail drawled, "I'd say you're *a lot* different."

"And I'd say that's quite the compliment." He raised his freshly filled sweet tea glass and clinked it to the edge of Abigail's. She decided not to mention that it hadn't been meant as a compliment. Weird or not, Gavin was all himself and she admired that—wished she could be more like it herself.

"So you like root canals and cats. What else?" she prompted, looking back toward the spot where his keys and that giant pink pom-pom had rested only minutes before.

"Well, you already know I like you. That makes three things," Gavin answered between sips of his tea.

Abigail frowned. She'd already told him everything worth knowing about her these days, and he still kept the better part of himself hidden. It didn't seem like a very good basis for rekindling their friendship. "Three things isn't a lot to go by when getting to know a person," she offered peaceably.

"But you already know me."

"Maybe, but that doesn't change the fact you're hiding something."

His smile faltered. "I'm not hiding. I just like to focus on the positive. Especially when you already have so much to be sad about without me heaping on."

"Gavin," she whispered. "What is it? You can tell me."

He ran both hands through his sandy blond hair before taking a deep breath and nodding. "I'll tell you, but I don't want to focus on it. I want this lunch to be about old friends reconnecting. Believe me, I spend enough time wallowing when I'm on my own."

She gulped, hating that she had brought his pain to the surface like this. She wouldn't have even guessed a single thing was wrong if not for his sudden change of demeanor. "You don't have to if—"

Gavin cleared his throat and set his glass back on the table, failing to make eye contact as he spoke. "No, I should. I need to get used to talking about it, and you've been so forthcoming with me. It's just…"

He snapped his line of vision back up to meet hers, and Abigail saw an intensity in his eyes she'd never seen before—not in all the times she'd spent mooning over those eyes in school and not in their time spent together as adults, either.

He regarded her silently before finally revealing, "As it turns out, you aren't the only one who's lost someone important to you."

CHAPTER 18

ABIGAIL

Abigail folded her hands in her lap and waited for Gavin to say more.

He closed his eyes and smiled as if picturing the most beautiful scene he could imagine behind his eyelids. "Her name was Millie—the little girl who gave me that keychain—and she was three years old at the time. She wasn't my daughter, but it sure felt like it. First I fell in love with her mother and then with Millie herself the moment we were introduced. Her mother, Susie, and I were set to be married that spring with little Millie serving as both the maid of honor and the flower girl. I couldn't have been happier if I tried."

He opened his eyes again and frowned at Abigail so deeply it made her heart ache for him, for the man he'd once been. "But then around about this time two years ago, Millie's father came back into the picture. And what could I say to save myself? He hadn't been the best to either of them, but he said he was a changed man, that he wanted the three of them to be a family."

"Oh gosh, Gavin, I'm so, so sorry." She hated when people apologized for things that weren't their fault, but what else could she say? Just like her, Gavin had loved and lost. Big time.

He smiled weakly before continuing. "Susie spent days weighing over the decision. Maybe even weeks. But in the end she decided that Millie needed her father and it would be best for all of us if I were to break off contact completely."

Abigail shook her head, unable to believe Gavin had gone from almost married with a family to depressingly single within the blink of an eye. "So that was it?" she asked gently. "You never saw them again?"

"They moved to a new state, wouldn't even tell me where, and I moved back to Charleston, opened my practice, and threw myself into work like there was nothing else that mattered. Because, really, there wasn't."

"I can't say I blame you." Abigail wished she had

the determination to keep working hard in the wake of her loss, but unlike Gavin, she'd lost the will to fight for herself.

"One day they were my whole world, and the next they were strangers. It was quite the shock to the system. It still hurts fresh as yesterday if I let it." He offered her a wistful smile. Even though no tears fell, Abigail couldn't help but wonder if they were ready and waiting. Or had Gavin simply reached the point where no more tears would come?

"That's why you reached out to me," she stated.

He nodded softly. "I needed a friend, too."

Abigail leaned across the table and clasped his hand. Was it worse that Susie chose to leave Gavin? That she intentionally cut him from her life, leading to not only loss but betrayal as well? Their situations weren't the same, but they certainly felt familiar to one another. Gavin had lost two people that meant everything to him, the poor guy.

"I'm happy to be your friend, but I don't know what to say to make it better," she admitted, finally understanding why people resorted to the same old platitudes over and over again. It felt better to say something cliché than to say nothing at all.

He sighed and gave her had a squeeze before

letting go. "That's the thing: words can't make it better. Only moving on does."

"Have you?" Abigail wanted to know. "Moved on?"

Gavin wrapped both hands around his half empty glass of tea. "I honestly don't know."

"Are you ready to?" She was pushing him now. She knew that, but somehow it felt as if curing Gavin would cure her as well, that it would prove recovery was at least possible. The problem was she had no idea what moving on past grief would even look like. Maybe there wasn't truly any way to ever really move on. Maybe you just buried your sadness underneath heaps of happier memories and prayed like heck that your pile wouldn't topple over.

Gavin shook his head—whether to say no or that he wasn't sure, Abigail couldn't figure out. Perhaps it didn't matter in the grand scheme of things.

"It sounds like you need a root canal," she said with a sly smile as she watched the waitress approach their table.

He laughed, the light returning to his eyes. "You're probably right about that. Root canals *do* make everything better. For now, though, I'll start with these." Gavin picked up his spoon and dipped it into his fresh bowl of shrimp and grits the moment the waitress set it in front of him.

"Thank you," Abigail said as she accepted her lunch as well.

They each savored their food in silence for a few moments before Gavin set his spoon down, wiped his mouth, and said, "It does help, you know. Throwing yourself into a project. My work keeps me sane, if not fully happy."

"I've been out of work for a while," she admitted. "It's hard to be creative without having that fire. I'm a graphic designer, by the way. In case I hadn't mentioned." She chose not to reveal her worry that her creative passion had been permanently doused, that it had left this world right alongside Owen.

"Doesn't need to be work," he answered between bites. "That's just what I chose. What about the puppies?"

The puppies. She'd only been away from them for a couple hours, but it seemed so much had happened since she left the house that morning. "I'm trying to find their owner but haven't had much luck yet. I also need to take them to the vet with my father this evening."

"I think they're your project," Gavin said with a genuine smile as he regarded her. "Haven't you felt better since your dad brought them home for you to look after?"

"A little," she said, pushing a particularly juicy shrimp around her bowl. "I like the dogs, but I don't want to get attached to them. You know how it is."

"I do. But I also know if you never let anyone in, then you can find yourself two years down the road every bit as broken as you are now."

He was right about that, and he clearly spoke from experience, too. It was easier to help the puppies who were here and needing her now. Little Owen still felt lightyears away. The puppies would be practically full grown by the time he was even born. Could they not only give her a head start on her parenting skills, but also help her heal on a deeper level? If Gavin was right, then yes. They absolutely could.

"Hey," Abigail protested halfheartedly. "I resemble that remark."

"Me too," Gavin answered with a wink before shoving another big bite in his mouth.

CHAPTER 19

ABIGAIL

After lunch, Abigail dropped Gavin back at his office and gave him a quick hug goodbye. "Thanks for everything," she whispered into his ear before they pulled apart. They exchanged numbers and promises to meet up for lunch sometime again soon, and then she made a quick stop off at the baby store before heading back home.

Hearing Gavin's tale of pain touched her in a way she hadn't expected. On the one hand, it was nice to know she had someone who could understand, someone other than her father who so desperately wanted to swoop in and fix everything for her.

On the other, it hurt her to see her friend hurting.

He'd seemed so carefree one moment and so tortured the next. Would she never truly escape her grief? Would it be like a shackle that remained forever bound to her ankle, sabotaging her as she tried to stumble her way through life?

There were no easy answers. That much hadn't changed.

She tried to push their lunch from her mind and focus on the aisle that stretched before her brimming with seemingly every infant knick-knack in existence. She pushed through to the clothing display and selected a dapper little outfit for Owen. It had soft overalls sewn into the onesie and even sported a little bowtie. He would look so handsome dressed to the nines while still comfy cozy in the soft cotton get-up.

Just five more months until he'd be here with her. She tried to picture it but couldn't quite form an image. Would he have a full shock of red hair like his papa? Or would his hair be dark and silky like Abigail's? He could be born bald as a cue ball for all she knew. One thing she knew for sure, though, was that he'd be hers.

All hers.

There was still so much to prep for his arrival, but at least now she knew she could do it. Gavin was proof that one could live with pain and still thrive in other ways. He'd seemed so normal and happy before he revealed his big secret to her. It obviously still hurt him, but it didn't stop him from reaching out to her, either.

But why her? Why Abigail of all people?

It was clear he wasn't looking for a relationship now that he'd told her the sad truth hidden behind that goofy grin. So what was he looking to accomplish, and why did he think she would be the one to get him there?

Maybe he was just well and truly lonely.

Or maybe, a small, niggling voice whispered in the back of her brain, *it wasn't an accident at all. Maybe God put you in each other's paths for a reason.*

She shook off the thought, not having the energy or desire to unpack it at the moment, and headed to the cash register to purchase little Owen's first outfit.

Back at home, Mama Mary whimpered and shook her teeny tail so furiously that her entire body followed right along with it.

"Did you miss me?" Abigail asked the dog with a

laugh, noticing Mary had knocked one of her puppies off the bed in her eagerness to greet her.

"Let's put you back, little Cookie," she told the pup, kissing the top of its head before nestling it in beside its brothers and sister. She headed to the kitchen to refill the mother Chihuahua's water dish, then fired up her laptop.

Mama Mary groaned and waited for Abigail to pick her up and place her on the bed beside her. The little dog gave Abigail a quick lick then dove under the covers, probably eager to have a nap completely undisturbed by her babies. Soon Abigail would understand how that went for herself—just five months to go.

She watched as Mama Mary got comfortable and fell asleep with a series of happy whimpers, then opened up Facebook and found that two messages were waiting for her.

The first was from Gavin: *Thank you for today. It meant a lot.*

Why me? she asked herself again. She'd asked herself that same question when Gavin had started paying attention to her in high school. He'd always been more popular than her, more handsome and well-liked by their peers. So what did he want with boring old Abigail? She had even less to offer now, but that didn't stop him from wanting to spend time together.

She'd need a while to think about how she wanted to respond, so she clicked on the other message. It read: *Hi, my name is Marcus Barnes, and I think you found my dog.*

CHAPTER 20

PASTOR ADAM

From the very second Abigail told me about this Marcus Barnes and his apparent claim to the dogs, my spidey sense started going haywire.

"Why won't he let us meet him at his house?" I asked her after she'd informed me that we had to go to meet Marcus instead of to the vet as planned.

She shrugged away my concern as if it were nothing. "I don't know, but I'm sure he has a good reason for it."

"Well, did he present evidence of a photographic or any other nature?"

She just rolled her eyes at me, same as she'd been doing since she was a little thing herself. "Dad, listen to you. You sound like Nancy Drew or something. Why would he say the dogs are his if they're not?"

That's what I wanted to know, too. Of course, I wouldn't keep our church dogs away from their rightful owner, but this smelled more than a little fishy if you asked me. And if Abigail wasn't going to worry about it, I'd have to worry about it enough for both of us. Luckily, I'd already started in on that particular task.

"Ready to go?" my daughter asked, carrying Mama Mary tucked tight into her chest and leaving the box of puppies for me to manage.

"As I'll ever be," I said with a grunt as I followed her out to the driveway and allowed her to drive us to the nearby Micky D's.

"You must be Marcus," Abigail said, striding right on up to a scraggly fella leaning up against an old GMC and smoking a cigarette.

Had she no sense of self-preservation?

Boy howdy, was it a good thing I'd talked her into letting me come along.

The man smiled in a way that told me he was

thinking unconscionable things about my daughter. He was lucky I was the turn the other cheek type and not the shoot now, ask questions later type. "Did you bring the dog?"

"Yes, we have her and the puppies in the car." Abigail wrung her hands, and I could tell this pained her, too.

"We need proof before we hand them over," I shot in. I loved that it was in my daughter's nature to trust people, but God had already told me that these dogs belonged to the church. And I trusted my God Almighty over a million such Marcus Barneses.

The man sniffed. "Proof? My word not enough for you?"

"Oh, no," Abigail said in a hurry. "We didn't mean to—"

"No, good sir, it is not," I said, taking a step forward and motioning for Abigail to get behind me just in case this turned ugly. "How do we know that the dog is yours? How do we know she'll be better off with you than with us? She was half dead when we found her, and that doesn't exactly inspire confidence in your pet-keeping skills."

"She's mine because I say she is." He puffed up his chest, then just as quickly deflated. "Look, her name is Sausage, and I was worried sick about her, all right? Can I just have my dog back?"

"You got any pictures of Sausage on your phone? Something you can show us?" I demanded.

"If you're looking to shake me down for a reward, it's not going to work. Just give me my dog."

"Well, this is quite the pickle, because I'm not giving you a single dog without proof, and you refuse to provide it."

"I'm not looking for a fight. I just want my dog back," the man said.

"And we just want to make sure we're doing right by these dogs, and right now sending them home with you doesn't seem like the right decision at all."

"So, what then? You're just going to refuse to give them to me?"

"Tell you what," I said with a smile. "We can divide them in half, that way we each get some. The mother dog stays with us, though."

"So you're telling me it's some dogs or none at all? You're crazy, man."

"So you choose none at all? Fine by us. C'mon, Abigail, let's go home."

"Wait!" Marcus said, trailing after us like he was the little lost puppy in this scenario. "Fine, I'll take half, if that's the way it's gotta be."

"Get in the car, Abigail," I said with a patient smile before turning back to Marcus and explaining with triumph, "We will not be giving you any puppies today."

"What?" the man exploded. He'd clearly had more than his fill of me, and I definitely felt the same way about him. "You just said you'd give me half."

"I did say that, and I'll also say this: you need to read your *Bible* more, son. You just let me get away with a classic King Solomon," I said, referencing the story about the two mothers fighting for the same baby. That time, the King had said they'd cut the child in half. I was just talking about dividing puppies, but still, if he loved that mama dog at all, he would not have settled for our split decision. And he would have had at least one photo to back up his ownership claims.

Marcus Barnes watched dumbfounded as I slipped into the car and motioned for Abigail to drive us back home, dogs in tow.

"I don't know what he was playing at," I told my daughter, "but I think I'll give Officer Jackson a call just to see if he can't find out for us."

CHAPTER 21

ABIGAIL

The vet was very understanding about rescheduling their appointment after Abigail's abrupt cancellation. A good thing, too, because it seemed her father had been right all along. Mama Mary and her puppies were meant to find them.

After returning home from their distressing meeting with Marcus Barnes, her father had put in a call to his friend in the county police department. The man hadn't been smart enough to use a fake name when reaching out to Abigail, so the police were able to track him down that same evening and bust his puppy mill operation wide open.

How one pregnant mother Chihuahua had managed to escape her cage and run all the way to their church was anyone's guess, but by doing so she'd saved her puppies and countless others, too.

"Would you mind keeping hold of the dogs a little longer?" Officer Jackson asked when he called to share the news. "The local animal shelter doesn't have enough room for all the dogs we took from this guy, and we need all the help we can get."

"Say no more," her father answered promptly. "Eternal Grace is on the case."

Abigail watched in amazement as her father started up the church phone tree, amassing more than a dozen volunteers in less than an hour. She hugged Mama Mary close to her chest, finally willing to admit how much the dog had come to mean to her in such a short span of time.

"Do you believe God sent us these dogs now?" her father asked, picking up each little pup in turn and giving it a gentle kiss on the head.

Abigail nodded, still clutching the mother dog tight. "I guess you were right about them being miracle workers. Mama Mary saved so many other dogs because of her bravery."

"And you helped her do it because of that strong sense of right and wrong you've had ever since you were a little girl." He came over to pet Mama Mary and make cooing noises at her. "You weren't going to rest until we found that owner."

"Thanks, Dad." She gave her father a hug and a kiss on the cheek, basking in her and Mary's shared victory. She had done something important, something miraculous, and it felt wonderful.

The next morning, the vet confirmed that they had rescued the dogs just in time. "They're all strong and healthy," she said, shaking her head in disbelief. "Even brief exposure to the cold at their age should have done them in. I just don't understand. It's like it's a—"

"Miracle?" her father finished with a knowing smile. "That's what I said."

The vet laughed before pressing her stethoscope to Mama Mary's chest. "Yes, I guess you could call it a miracle. Someone was clearly looking out for these dogs."

"How's Mary doing? Is she healthy, too?" Abigail asked from her seat in the corner. Even though she still wasn't sure how she felt about God these days, she'd prayed for that little dog hard and long. Mary had overcome too much to not get her happily ever after now.

The vet frowned briefly before putting on a placating smile. "Yes, she appears healthy. But she's had litters before. It's hard to say how many, though I'd guess she was being bred nonstop since reaching sexual maturity."

"How old is she now?" Abigail chewed her lip nervously.

The vet shifted her stethoscope to Mary's back and listened in a couple different spots before turning her attention back to Abigail. "My best guess is three."

"Only three!" her father sputtered, his brows lifted in surprise. "She sure has seen a lot for her short time on earth."

The poor dog had suffered three years of captivity and forced breeding, three years of non-stop torment, Abigail realized. *So why does she trust me? She shouldn't trust anyone.*

"She's remarkably well-adjusted for what she's been through," the vet continued, confirming just what Abigail had been thinking.

"She's a hero," Abigail said, picking Mama Mary off the exam table and giving her a kiss between the ears. This amazing creature had chosen her. Perhaps she'd seen something in Abigail that Abigail had yet to discover in herself.

"So what next?" she asked the vet, eager to make their adoption of the church dogs official. She was never letting a single one of them out of her sight again—not if she could help it.

"We'll take up a collection at church to help pay for the veterinary care of the others who were rescued from the mill," her father said.

"And I'll perform those exams at cost," the vet added. "A rescue this size is a huge undertaking, but I can see the dogs are in great hands." She reached out to shake both of their hands before picking up her stack of folders and leaving them alone in the exam room.

"Praise the Lord," her father said. "We couldn't have asked for better news today."

"Are you really taking up a collection?" Abigail mumbled, not sure why she was surprised by this news.

"Of course." He smiled and puffed out his chest, always so proud of his church and the people who made up its family. "The congregation will want to help."

"*I* want to help," she said before she could change her mind. She still had a rough relationship with God, but she wanted to do her part to make the world better, to help in whatever way she could.

He gave her the side eye. "Does that mean you'll come to church this Sunday?"

"I could design flyers, or—"

"Or you could finally come back to church." He turned his full gaze on her, a warm smile took over his entire face. "Come tell everyone about the dogs and why they need help. Introduce them to Mama Mary and her pups. Maybe say hello to God while you're visiting His house."

"Okay," she said before taking a deep, shaky breath. "I'm in."

CHAPTER 22

ABIGAIL

Abigail texted Gavin to update him on the puppy mill bust, their vet visit, and her upcoming return to church. Almost immediately after she pressed send, her phone buzzed with an incoming call.

"Wow," Gavin said, not even bothering with hello. "All that in the space of twenty-four hours? You definitely don't do anything halfway."

"I guess not," she answered with a laugh.

Mama Mary cocked her head to the side as if trying to listen in to the conversation, which only caused Abigail to laugh harder.

"So you get to keep the dogs?" Gavin asked. Hope filled his voice, and the sound of a whirring drill accompanied it as well.

"Are you…? Are you doing a root canal while talking to me?"

"Maybe a little bit. I have you on speaker," he confessed without sounding the least bit apologetic.

"Gavin!" she shouted, plopping down onto her bed with a soft whoosh as the down repositioned itself in her comforter. "That's awful. You need to be one-hundred percent present for that. Your poor patient is probably terrified."

A muffled moan came from the other end of the call, and she couldn't tell whether it was the patient's way of expressing pain, terror, or laugher.

"Oh, *sure*," Gavin joked, drawing out that last word an unnatural length.

She could just picture him rolling his eyes, and it made her feel light and easy despite all the awful things that had happened in her life the past few months. They said that time healed all wounds, but sometimes it felt like going back in time was the only way to move forward. Perhaps that was why she was so sentimental, as Gavin had deftly pointed out.

"It's not like I've done a million of these before, but okay. Have it your way," he said with a dramatic and clearly faked sigh. "By the way, I'll be there with you and the dogs on Sunday, too. Okay, bye!"

He hung up before she could protest, presumably

returning his full attention to his latest root canal victim.

Okay, well, I guess that's that.

She'd be seeing Gavin again on Sunday. Perhaps his presence would make the visit a little easier on her. Now she just needed to find a way to fill her time between now and then. It was only Tuesday, after all, and Sunday seemed a mighty long way off.

She leaned back against her headboard and let out a long, beleaguered sigh.

Mama Mary popped up from her bed and trotted over. Her petite paws hugged the edge of the mattress as she whined and begged for Abigail to pick her up.

"You can save fifty-seven dogs from a puppy mill, but you can't even jump onto the bed," Abigail said with a chuckle as she lifted the Chihuahua into her arms. Mary's triumphs and challenges spoke to Abigail in a way little else had. Even though the small things were hard, that didn't stop her from achieving big—some might say impossible—feats. Could that be a lesson for Abigail's own life? And for Gavin's, too?

"You know what?" Abigail told her canine friend. "I think I'll draw you. Stay there," she said, petting the little dog who was still trying to get comfortable on the bed. "I'll be right back."

The very moment Abigail got up, however, Mama Mary thumped down onto the floor after her and waddled down the hall right at her heels.

Most of Abigail's work had been digital over the past decade, but right now, returning to the basics appealed to her more than she could say. Her drawing charcoals had been tucked away in her old bedroom years ago, which meant she'd need to visit the abandoned shrine to her youth in order to claim them.

Everything sat just as she remembered it—white wood furniture, pink walls, and princess murals. Her mother had designed this room for her, which is why she'd never wanted to change it even as she grew up and her tastes changed. It was the beginning of the sentimentality that Gavin so admired in her. But really, she was afraid to let go of anything, not knowing if there would be a way to ever get it back.

This room would need to be converted into little Owen's nursery, she realized. It was the only spare room they had in the whole house. And it had sat unoccupied long enough.

Maybe her old bedroom set could make some other little girl happy, could turn her bedroom into a fairy wonderland as it had done for Abigail. It wasn't right to keep things to herself if they could help others. She'd always known that. Her father had instilled a sharp sense of morality in her, even if he was partially to blame for her inability to move on past the... well, *past*.

After all, he'd never dated, never remarried, and to her knowledge had never tried to find her mother after she'd left them both behind. Did she know she was about to become a grandmother? Was she even still alive?

Abigail hadn't the slightest clue, but she needed to stop focusing on the things she couldn't change, the things she couldn't have. Right now, she would grab tight to that tiny flicker of creativity Mama Mary had inspired and see if she could coax it into something bigger.

First she'd draw the best picture of her dog she could manage, and then she'd see about conquering other mountains.

CHAPTER 23

ABIGAIL

Sunday morning arrived even faster than Abigail had dared to hope. True to his word, Gavin stood waiting outside the front doors wearing a light gray suit and an expectant smile. It reminded her of that ninth grade dance all over again. Only this time she was wearing a pair of stretchy pants and a stretchy tunic style shirt. Her thick hair was pulled into a messy bun and hiding a huge tangle she'd been unable to comb out that morning.

Yes, unfortunately, pregnancy had made her always thick hair nightmarish and almost impossible to care for these days. At least her skin had remained smooth and blemish free, with only a few extra hairs poking through on her chin as a result of all those blasted hormones.

"You look beautiful," Gavin said, holding the door open for her and Mama Mary who walked at her side on a leash.

Abigail couldn't help but laugh at that one. "Thanks," she said with a goofy grin that mirrored the one Gavin so often bestowed upon her.

"What?" he asked, following in after her. "What did I do wrong?"

"Nothing," she assured him. "It's good to see you. I just feel a mite underdressed."

Gavin waved her off. "Nah, you're the pastor's daughter. You set the standard for fashion around here, if I remember correctly."

She laughed again, already thankful that he'd insisted on accompanying them to service today. "I'm not sure you do, but I'll take it."

"Hey, where are the puppies?" Gavin asked, searching around as if their carrier would materialize out of thin air.

"Back in my father's office. That way they can be with their mom between services, and nobody gets too hungry."

They stepped through the double doors into the sanctuary, and it felt as if all eyes had turned on them. Everyone was probably looking at Mama Mary, but Abigail couldn't help but feel scrutinized—judged—

by the eager glances so many sent straight in their direction.

"Honey, up here!" her father called, jumping and waving his arms from near the pulpit.

Oh brother, she thought while hurrying over to her father as fast as her swollen feet would carry her.

"Morning, Gavin," her father said with a curt nod before wrapping Abigail in his arms and squeezing her tight.

"What are you doing?" Abigail hissed in her father's ear. "You literally just saw me five minutes ago in the car."

His smile didn't dampen one bit. He even winked at her to further punctuate his point. "I'm just happy to have you here. Back in church where you belong."

"Don't get used to it," she warned.

"What, me?" he asked, pretending to be taken aback. *"Never."*

The band chose that moment to start the music up, and her father motioned for them to sit right in the front row. If Mama Mary was startled by the loud instruments, she sure didn't show it. She sat proudly by Abigail's feet, thumping her little tail to the beat.

Abigail sang the words she knew so well as she glanced around the sanctuary she'd all but grown up inside. Last time she was here, white flowers had lined every surface and Owen's closed casket had been draped with a neat, unblemished United States flag. She'd hardly been able to stand as the officers had folded it up into a neat triangle and offered it to her, thanking her for her husband's service and for her own sacrifice.

Today the only flowers were leftover poinsettias from Christmas. Everything was bright, upbeat, and happy, but that didn't change the fact that people received their last rites here, that this church saw marriages that were doomed to fail, new lives that would end all too early… so much suffering.

Looking around on that cool Sunday morning, you would never guess that these four walls had seen so much pain, witnessed so many tragedies. It was just like Gavin and that goofy grin of his—pretty on the outside, but broken on the inside.

Was that all she could aspire to now? The veneer of happiness? Of fullness?

The band switched to a new song and—just like that—Abigail felt like she was going to be sick. She ran out of the sanctuary, Mary waddling along quickly at her heels. It wasn't morning sickness, but something else—the sudden violence of a horrible memory overtaking her system. In that moment it felt as if she were reliving the funeral all over again.

Why had she come today? She wasn't ready to be here yet. Maybe she never would be, and maybe that would be okay. Her father could teach little Owen about God and Jesus and just leave her out of it.

Mary stood on her hind legs and pawed Abigail's knees, a knowing look in her little charcoal eyes.

"I'll be okay," she told the dog. "It's just silly human stuff. You wouldn't understand."

She bent down to pet the sweet Chihuahua when an odd sensation stopped her mid-motion. She remained perfectly still, waiting to see if it would happen again.

That was when Gavin burst through the doors and rushed over to her side. "Are you okay?" he whisper-yelled. "You had me worried there."

She held up a hand and—

There it was again!

"Gavin," she cried, forgetting the need to remain silent. "Come quick!"

In an instant, he was at her side. Tears flowed freely as she reached for his hand and pressed it up against her abdomen.

And then it happened again.

And again.

"Oh my gosh, is that?" Gavin asked, his eyes shining as he stared at her belly in wonder.

"Little Owen says hello," she sobbed. "That was the first time I felt him kick."

"He must like it here," Gavin said with a cajoling smile. And even though he was teasing, Abigail knew he was absolutely, one-hundred percent right.

CHAPTER 24

ABIGAIL

When the music stopped playing, Abigail dragged both Gavin and Mama Mary back into the sanctuary. "I'm supposed to go on at the end of the announcements, and they come right after praise and worship. Let's go!"

Her father caught her eye from his place behind the pulpit and motioned for her to join him upfront. "Ladies and gentleman of the Eternal Grace congregation," he drawled. His Southern always came out in extra measure when he was before an audience. "I'd like to welcome my daughter, Abigail, to the pulpit along with a special guest she'll introduce to y'all shortly."

The crowd of church goers gasped and cooed as

Mama Mary proudly pranced down the center aisle at Abigail's side. Gavin walked with them until he reached his seat in the front row and plopped right down into it.

That meant the rest of this was up to Abigail now.

Her father gave her a quick hug and kiss, then went to take a seat of his own to the side of the pulpit.

"Hi, everyone," she said into the little microphone that was hooked onto the wooden stand. The resulting feedback told her she'd leaned in too close.

The crowd that stretched out before her continued to smile expectantly. Most still had their eyes fixed on Mama Mary.

I can do this, Abigail told herself. *It's important.*

"Hi, everyone," she started again. "I'm Abigail Sutton-Elliott. Pastor Adam's my dad. Um, I know you guys haven't seen me in a while, and for that I'm sorry. I'm back today, though, with important news. Good news. And a plea for your help."

Murmurs rose from the sea of congregants before her.

She looked to her father who nodded encouragingly and motioned for her to continue. With a deep breath, she bent down to pick up her doggie companion and hold her as high above the pulpit as she could manage.

"This is Mama Mary, and she's my hero," she told everyone. "If you have children in the Sunday school class—or if you're part of the Eternal Grace phone tree—you may already know part of her story. Here's the full thing." Abigail paused to take a deep, measured breath.

Gavin gave her the thumbs up, and she felt grateful again that he had come to support her today. Public speaking had never been a strength of hers—not like it was for her father. But maybe her passion for these pups would get her through it. After all, they were counting on her.

"Mama Mary escaped from a puppy mill during that huge snow storm on Christmas Eve," she continued, pausing to make eye contact with several members of the audience. "She was very pregnant at the time and actually came to our nativity scene to have her puppies that night."

She paused again while a gasp swept through the crowd.

"She had four little pups, who are all doing fine by the way, and my dad—Pastor Adam—found them before they could suffer too badly from the cold. They've been with us ever since, and earlier this week, we found out about the puppy mill Mama Mary escaped from. The police did a bust up and found a total of fifty-seven dogs being kept in just horrible conditions."

Her voice cracked, and she grew angry just thinking about what all those poor dogs had been through. How anyone could treat animals so cruelly… well, it proved that there was evil in this world just as much as there was good. She glanced to her father again, who was also wiping away a small, glistening tear.

"That's why I'm here to talk with you today. These dogs need our help. Some of you have already volunteered space in your homes. Mama Mary and I are here to ask that you reach deep into your hearts and give whatever amount you can to contribute to the veterinary care and to finding forever homes for each of these fifty-seven dogs."

The ushers rose and distributed the collection plates to the rows in front and back, and the band began to play soft music behind her.

Emboldened, Abigail stepped out from behind the pulpit so that everyone could see Mama Mary clearly. She raised her voice loud enough to reach the folks all the way in the back and then promised, "I also want you to know that Mama Mary and her puppies aren't going anywhere. Ever since my father found them, he knew God had sent them for our church. At first I didn't believe him, but then I got to know Mary and her puppies. And I remembered just what my father is capable of achieving when he puts his faith in the Almighty."

Laughter rose up from the congregation. They all knew her father every bit as well as she did. They loved him like she did, too.

"So I don't know everything yet," she continued with a smile of gratitude, "but I do know Mary and her four pups—Cookie, Brownie, Cupcake, and Muffin—will be around for years to come, to help our church in whatever way we need. Thank you."

Abigail gave another quick smile before she crept back to her seat beside Gavin who put his arm around her.

"Good job," he whispered.

And she believed him, too.

CHAPTER 25

PASTOR ADAM

Let me tell you just how proud I was of my baby girl that Sunday. I knew she had a hard time facing the Maker, and she'd always struggled with speaking in front of crowds, too—but that didn't stop her from coming through for those pups.

Everyone clapped as she took her seat. Me loudest of all.

Now it was my turn to speak out about something that was important to me. Despite all my hoping and praying, I knew I might not get another chance to deliver a sermon to my daughter, at least not anytime soon. So this one would have to count extra.

With a quick adjustment of my tie, I rose to take

my spot behind the pulpit. Most of my sermons as of late had been about the Fruits of the Spirit, and my flock was no doubt expecting more of the same, but today I decided to depart from my carefully planned lecture series and speak to a topic I knew Abigail would be able to relate to beyond any shadow of a doubt—and that was our church dogs.

"Isn't my daughter beautiful, folks?" I asked, assuming my position at the front of the church, and was met with a ripple of approval through the sanctuary.

My darling daughter slid further down in her chair as if that would be enough to hide her. Well, she had to get used to people looking at her, admiring her, because much more of that would be coming soon.

"I'm so grateful to her that she introduced y'all to Mama Mary and told you her story, because Abigail is absolutely right. These pups are going to be with our church for a long time to come. Jesus said let the little children come to me, and that's just what this litter of pups did. They found Him in His church. *They found us.*" I paused here as I was apt to do whenever I needed a point to sink in deep.

"God has always been willing to use anyone and anything He can to get our attention, and this time

He chose a litter of little dogs—of mini miracles—to deliver His message.

"Hmm, okay. So what might that message be?" I cocked my head to the side just like Mama Mary did whenever she was paying extra close attention to Abigail. "Well, let me ask you this: what message do you need to hear?"

Most people laughed. A few looked uncomfortable. Those were the ones I decided to focus on. Sometimes I prepared my sermons word for word to make sure I got them just right. Others, I played it by ear. Today was an *other* kind of day.

"We're all searching for something in this life—all praying, wishing, desperately hoping for that one thing that can change us and our lives for the better. What's *your* one thing? Take a moment to think about that, because we'll be coming back to it later."

I glanced toward Abigail who was nodding along without even realizing it. I knew her one thing because it was the same as mine—to put the grief aside, to stitch up our broken hearts, and learn to survive without our other halves. I wanted that for Abigail even more than I wanted it for myself. After all, I'd been living with my mess of a heart for years, and if I could spare my daughter that same fate, I'd consider myself a blessed man.

God could do it. He could do it for both of us.

"Got your one thing?" I asked the congregation.

They nodded, shouted yes, just generally expressed their readiness to hear what came next.

"Good," I said, letting that one word echo through the sanctuary a couple times before continuing on. "Now I bet it feels too big, too far, too heavy, but you know what? *If you have faith as small as a mustard seed, nothing—nothing!—will be impossible for you.* Wow… Do you know how small a mustard seed is?" I held my fingers in a circle so tiny hardly a speck of light filtered through. "Even smaller than that. Wow."

"Now look at this tiny dog," I said, walking over to Abigail and grabbing Mama Mary's leash so that I could trot her across the front of the sanctuary. "She's a Chihuahua. That's the smallest kind of dog in the whole wide world. She was pregnant—just about to give birth, as a matter of fact. She'd been kept in a cage her whole life. She'd been tormented, neglected, forgotten… but not by God."

I stooped down to pick that brave mama dog up and into my arms. "God gave her a strength she couldn't have had on her own. He guided her paws out of that prison and straight to His house where she and her pups would be safe. Now if God can make that time to save a little dog, what might He be willing to do for his own children? For you, brothers and sisters?"

A pause here gave everyone a bit more time to think before I asked with a humble smile, "How big—how impossible—does your one thing seem now?"

Various murmurs rose up over the congregation, but I wasn't done yet.

"I can do all things through Christ who strengthens me," I quoted from the scripture. "Not some things. All things! Not a few things..." I paused to allow my church to supply the answer.

"All things!" they cried in unison.

I smiled and nodded. "All things. Imagine that. *All things* in Christ."

When I glanced back over to my daughter, she was still nodding along, but now she was crying big, fat tears, and I didn't know whether they were joyful—or if I'd somehow pushed her even deeper into the depths of despair.

All things, I reminded myself. *Including helping my daughter to heal. Amen.*

CHAPTER 26

ABIGAIL

Abigail raced out of the sanctuary for the second time during that same service. With a quick hand gesture, she motioned for Gavin to stay behind as she tore a path to her father's office with Mama Mary following closely behind. As soon as she shut the door securely behind her, she placed the excited mother dog into the box with her puppies.

She didn't mean to run off, but she needed a few minutes on her own, and she needed a break from her father's hard-hitting words. He'd spoken right to the heart of her every fear. He'd said that God took time out to help Mama Mary and her litter, which was great… except that didn't change the fact He'd chosen to deny Owen that same protective care.

What made one life more important than the other?

Her father claimed she could do anything with a little bit of faith, and she'd memorized the verses he cited long ago as a Sunday school student—but today she considered them in a new light. Was she willfully remaining broken by slamming her heart's door to God?

She wished she knew. Oh, how she wished she knew.

Little Owen woke up and kicked her from the inside. What did he feel? What was he trying to communicate to her now? And why did it feel that everyone—even her unborn child and a handful of miraculous Chihuahuas—knew God better than she did?

"Owen," she whispered, not sure whether she was speaking to her husband or her child. Maybe she was saying something they both needed to hear. "I feel so lost. Like I'm standing just outside of where I need to be, but there's this big giant wall blocking me from going in. How do I tear down that wall when I don't have any strength left to fight?" she sobbed.

The door creaked open behind her and her father's voice floated in sure and strong. "Don't you remember the story of Jericho?"

She kept her back to him so he wouldn't see her patchy face. "Dad…"

"If you're already there, all you need to do is march. And maybe blow a trumpet if you have one." He crossed the room and took a seat on top of his desk, forcing her to look at him.

"This is serious," Abigail argued. What was he doing here with her? Shouldn't he still be preaching? Or had she really let so much time pass her by without noticing?

"I know, baby girl." He sighed and leaned forward with his hands on either knee. "I'm proud of you for coming today. Just know this: you don't have to figure it all out at once. To be honest, even I haven't got it all figured out yet."

This was not what Abigail needed to hear. It already felt impossible, carrying on, being happy again. For her father to tell her that the answers would come little by little—if at all—dimmed her hope even further.

"Then how can you tell others what to believe?" she needed to know. "How can you stand up there week after week telling others how to live a good life when you admit that you haven't figured it out yet?"

"It's not *me*. It's God speaking through me. And if you'll listen, He'll speak to you. If you let him, He'll speak through you. Just like He's doing with those dogs."

Abigail crossed her arms over her chest. He was always so predictable. Yes, he loved her, but his answers never wavered. He always, always brought it back to God.

"Why are you so sure these dogs were meant for us? They're just dogs," she said, feeling guilty even before the words had fully left her mouth.

"Faith like a mustard seed," he said with a nod and the start of a smile. "But here's a secret: if you don't have a whole mustard seed, that's okay, too. Take that half seed, that quarter seed, that one billionth of a seed, and water it. See what God can do then."

Did she have one billionth of a seed? Perhaps somewhere deep down in a part of her that she'd boarded up to protect from pain. But could it really be enough? Could something new grow from such a tiny fragment?

She shook her head and turned her face away so her father wouldn't see her frown. "You claim it's a miracle they found us, but what if it's just a coincidence? A freak accident even?"

"If it is, then it is," her father answered, surprising her for once as he placed a hand over his heart. "But I choose to believe in miracles. The world looks more beautiful that way. You don't have to be right to be happy. Think about that."

She cracked a small smile. This line of reasoning she could relate to. It didn't require her to sort through her feelings about God first. At last it gave her a place to start. "Are you saying ignorance is bliss?" she asked.

He cleared his throat and loosened his tie. It always ended up a mess by the end of his second service. He hated wearing that thing, but still he donned it some time or another every single Sunday.

"No, what I'm saying is I know you're struggling with God's decision to call Owen home," he offered gently. "You want to understand why, but maybe you *can't* understand. Maybe none of us can. So where does that leave you? Well, you can torture yourself trying to figure it out, or you can trust that God is good, that He loves you, and that He's got a plan."

"That somehow involves Chihuahuas?" Abigail asked with a smile. Although it sometimes annoyed her, his unwavering faith also provided a constant in a world that felt like a dizzying blur even at the best of times.

"Why, yes, I believe it does." He rose from the desk and straightened to full height, looking down the bridge of his nose at Abigail who was still folded in on herself. "And what do you believe?"

"I don't know," she admitted. And then after a pause, added, "And maybe this time, that's okay. Thank you, Dad. I love you."

"I love you, too, baby girl." His entire face lit up just as it always had whenever she told him she loved him. He'd tucked her in every night of her childhood, exchanged butterfly kisses and "I love you's" every single time, but still—still—hearing that affirmation from her meant the world to him. It meant the world to her, too. *Thank God for loving fathers.*

"And you know what else?" he asked.

"What?" Abigail asked, allowing him to pull her to his chest in a gentle hug.

"I don't think the Chihuahuas are the only miracle that found us this Christmas season." He smiled down at her, waiting to see if she'd been able to interpret his latest cryptic burst of gratitude.

She had not. "What do you mean?"

"I'll leave you to figure that out on your own," he said as he departed toward the door. "I've got a second sermon to deliver."

CHAPTER 27

ABIGAIL

Abigail stayed with Mama Mary and her pups until it was time to deliver her plea to the second service crowd. She was surprised to find that Gavin had waited for her despite her sudden departure.

"You okay?" he whispered as she took a seat beside him at the end of praise and worship.

She smiled and nodded. Shortly after, her father called her to the stage and she spoke with every bit as much passion as she had the first time, maybe even a little bit more… and then she was ready to go home. She'd faced more than enough for one day—especially after the emotionally draining talk with her father in his office.

"Need me to drive you home?" Gavin asked, leaning in to her when she returned to his side.

"Please," she whispered, grabbing his hand and leading both him and Mary back to the office to retrieve the puppies.

"You were gone for a while," he said, concern knitting his brow. "I would have come to find you if I knew where to look."

"No, it's okay." Abigail brushed a strand of loose hair behind her ear and picked up the box of squirmy Chihuahua babies. "I needed a little bit of time after…" She let her words trail off and made a rolling hand gesture instead.

"Yeah, that was something, all right." Gavin sucked in a deep breath, filling his chest and lifting his shoulders, then let it out again slowly. "It's been so long since my family changed churches, I guess I'd forgotten how great your father is at what he does."

That, she couldn't deny. People loved her father for a reason. She loved him for many reasons of her own, too. One of them was that he was always willing to say what needed to be said, even and especially when it was hard.

"Yeah," she said with a smile. "And that particular bout of preaching was meant for me, so it was a lot to take in."

"You're really lucky, you know," he said, taking the box from her but remaining close as he spoke softly. His sandy hair fell over his brows as he leaned in. "You're surrounded by love on all sides. Even the inside."

Gavin's goofy grin darted across his face before he turned serious again. "You're a special woman, Abigail, and sometimes it seems you're the only one who doesn't know that."

She forced a laugh, but Gavin held her eyes with his, refusing to treat his words as a joke. "How can you say that when we haven't known each other that long?" she asked.

Gavin cocked his head to the side, but kept his focus intently on her. "Haven't we?"

Abigail's cheeks grew warm. All of her grew warm. "I meant as adults."

"The core of who we are doesn't change, Abigail Elliott-Sutton, and you've always been beautiful in absolutely every sense of the word." He drew closer still, bending briefly to set the box aside before taking her in his arms.

"Gavin," she murmured into his shoulder. "I can't."

"I'm not asking for anything," he said. "I just want you to know that I'm here. I'm close. I'm ready to go to bat for you in whatever way you need. Right now, I know that's just as a friend, but maybe someday there will be a way for us to mean more to each other. I know you'll need a long time to heal, to find yourself again, but I'm not going anywhere. Do you understand?"

She nodded, unable to say anything in that moment. "I do," she choked out at last. This she understood. It was faith that had become a mystery to her, but love made perfect sense. Had Gavin really carried a torch for her all these years, or did the broken part of him fit together with the broken part of her?

She wanted to believe she could love him one day, but right now she honestly didn't know how her heart could ever make space for any man other than Owen.

Gavin's chest beat beneath her cheek and for a moment she let herself believe it was Owen's. The two men's hearts beat out the same tempo until Owen's had suddenly stopped.

What if she allowed herself to fall for Gavin, only to lose him, too?

Loving Gavin was terrifying, but so was not loving him. She felt as if she'd gotten stuck in an impossible place. Maybe she had.

Gavin pulled away, placing a hand on each of her

shoulders and holding her at arm's length. "I'm not trying to scare you, and I'm not trying to saddle you with anything more than you can handle. I need time to heal, too, but ever since you came back into my life, I finally feel like I have a reason to try, to open myself back up again. I just want you to know that. Even if you don't feel the same way now, even if you never feel the same way, I just need you to know what's in my heart."

"Thank you, Gavin," she said, unable to add anything more. What was right in this situation? She'd loved Gavin before, but that was years ago—practically a whole lifetime. He said the core of who you are doesn't change, but what if he was wrong?

The only thing she knew for sure is that she needed some time by herself to figure things out.

God. Gavin. Everything.

CHAPTER 28

ABIGAIL

Abigail spent the rest of that day on her own. Neither her father nor Gavin pushed her for anything more. Instead, both thankfully left her to rest and recover from the tough conversations that had taken place in her father's tiny church office.

So, to pass the time, she finished reading the romantic adventure book she'd downloaded for free and immediately bought the next in the series. She also drew another picture of Mama Mary and just generally gave herself permission to relax for a change.

One afternoon stretched into two, which quickly became three. The monotony was at last broken when the puppies finally opened their beautiful eyes and looked into Abigail's for the very first time. She'd admit she cried, but then again, she always cried these days.

Now that the pups had open ears and eyes, they became feistier than ever. Mama Mary was no longer able to wander away and hide to take a nap on her own. Tending to the puppies became a full-time job now that they were moving toward independence and able to uncover heaps of trouble if not watched constantly.

To celebrate, Abigail decided to take the pups to a park for their first big outdoor adventure since that fateful Christmas Eve rescue. It didn't take her long, though, to realize her mistake. There was no way she could handle all four puppies and their mom at once.

She needed help.

But when she called her father to ask for him to meet her at the park—so that the trip wouldn't be a total bust—he said he'd been called in for a last-minute meeting at the church and suggested she call Gavin instead.

Abigail thought about that one for a few minutes before deciding to act. She'd been putting off Gavin's texts since his confession of love for her, and while she missed him, she just didn't know how to act casual in his company either. After a bit of hurried deliberation, she decided to head home on her own rather than requesting that Gavin join her at the park.

When she arrived back at her father's house, however, Gavin's oversized truck stood waiting in the driveway. Unfortunately, Southern manners dictated she welcome him warmly rather than driving around the block a few times until he gave up and went away.

She cursed under her breath, put on her best smile, and ambled over to meet him with all five Chihuahuas nipping at her heels.

"Hi Gavin," she called, offering a small wave. "What a nice surprise."

He raised an eyebrow. "Is it?" he asked. "Because someone's been avoiding my texts all week."

"Well… I've been busy with the puppies, is all."

"Uh huh." He looked as if he wanted to hug her but thankfully held himself back.

Despite the awkwardness of this unplanned meeting, she had missed talking with him these past few days—missed seeing him, too. But how could she admit that without leading him on? Everything would be that much harder now the she knew he had feelings for her. She couldn't just get over her husband's death in a matter of months. It wouldn't be fair to Owen, but expecting Gavin to ignore his emotions and them relegating him to the role of a simple friendship wouldn't be fair to him.

So what was fair to Abigail, and—?

"I know what you're thinking," Gavin said with that goofy grin she found so much comfort in.

"Sorry," she muttered, all the while wondering: *Does he actually know? Am I that obvious?*

"You're not the one who needs to apologize," he said with a frown. "I put a lot of pressure on you the other day when that was the last thing I wanted to do."

"Gavin, stop, you don't have to—"

"Yes," he said pointedly. *"I do.* I owe you an apology, and I've also brought a peace offering. A deal, too, if you're willing to make it."

Okay, he definitely had her attention now. She waited to see what he would say or do next.

"Do you want the gift or the deal first?" he asked as a mischievous smile stretched from one cheek to the other.

"Umm…" She thought about it but had no idea what either could be, which made it impossible to choose. She'd always been bad about making choices, no matter how frivolous. And somehow she doubted this one was.

"Too slow!" Gavin cried, slapping the back of his

truck. "You're getting the gift. Think you can grab the door for me?"

She ran back to the porch and opened first the screen door and then the heavy wooden front door. The small herd of Chihuahuas trotted merrily into the house. When she glanced back to the driveway again, she found Gavin struggling with a long piece of honey-colored wood.

"Gavin Holbrook," she scolded, placing her free hand on her hip "What did you do?"

"I told you that already. I got you a gift," he said after triumphantly extracting the furniture piece from his truck bed.

"That doesn't look like a small token of apology."

"Well, *small* is what you make of it. Right, Mama Mary?" he said to the dog who had come back outside to supervise the undertaking and now stood beside Gavin as if she, too, was in on the surprise.

"Does that work both ways?" Abigail asked, hardly able to suppress a laugh. "Because I don't think it does."

Gavin winked at her as he carried the first piece past her and through the open doors. "A friend of mine makes custom furniture, and he's been having a rough go of things lately," he explained with his back to her. "I figured this could be a great gift for you as well as a way to help him. Besides, you need one."

"What?" she asked as he brushed past her to return to his truck for a second trip.

"It's a crib," he said before, stretching over to grab more pieces. "Tommy offered to deliver it in one piece, but I don't know. I kind of wanted us to build it together. I hope that's okay." He popped back up and gave her a cautious smile.

"That's more than okay, Gavin. Thank you so much. This is a wonderful gift." Her heart warmed as she pictured the two of them fitting together the pieces to build something wonderful for little Owen.

He let out a big sigh of relief, then jumped right back into teasing her. "If you like this, just wait until you find out about the deal."

CHAPTER 29

ABIGAIL

Abigail watched from her perch by the door as Gavin brought in the last of the crib pieces. She liked having him here, liked being taken care of again—but was that enough to risk her heart a second time and so soon after her first love ended in utter heartbreak?

"Well, where should we build it?" Gavin asked, wiping a bead of sweat from his forehead as he surveyed the already filled living room with a befuddled expression.

She latched the door shut and stepped back into the house. Puppies ran around like crazy. Clearly the short period without supervision had already yielded significant damage. Little Muffin even tried to fit his mouth around a piece of the crib before Gavin shooed him off.

"I want to give the baby my pink room, but it's still filled with all my old things," she answered. "And I haven't had the chance to paint it yet, either. I doubt my little boy will appreciate all the pink princess decor that's in there."

"Well, c'mon then, we've got a lot of work to do." Gavin charged toward her old room, still remembering where it was after all these years—or maybe just getting lucky with his choice of doors.

"Gavin, wait!" Abigail hobbled after him. "We can't just set up the nursery right now."

He blinked twice. "Why not?"

She stared back at him blankly, completely unable to come up with an appropriate excuse.

Gavin smiled and tilted his head back. "Yup, that's what I thought," he said with a laugh. "Do you know what you want to do with all the old furniture?"

"I was thinking of donating it," she mumbled, standing in the doorway as he appraised each piece of furniture.

"Perfect. I have my truck, and it should all fit, so let's take it straight out." He pulled the mattress off the bed and set it against the wall. "Actually, wait. You shouldn't be lifting anything in your condition. Or smelling paint fumes, for that matter," he pointed out. "I guess I'll handle things in here. You rest."

"All I ever do is rest," Abigail admitted. "I want to help."

He glanced over his shoulder with a sinful smile. "Well, I wouldn't say no to a tall glass of iced tea, if you happen to have any just lying around."

She gasped and lifted a hand to her chest, playing her part of this charade perfectly. "Shut your mouth. You know Dad and I have always make it fresh."

"Then hop to, darling, while I take care of business in here." He winked and made a clicking noise before turning his attention back to the furniture.

Of course, maybe Abigail should have protested at least a little, but then again, she liked this playful, teasing side of Gavin. It made things easier between them, which is what they both sorely needed right now.

After fixing a glass of tea for Gavin and some lemonade for herself, she took off her shoes and padded back into her old bedroom. Gavin had already managed to clear the dresser and nightstand out, leaving the room emptier than she'd ever seen it in her entire life. It was truly amazing how quickly the remnants of a life could be removed, replaced.

Gavin drained half of his beverage in a single gulp, then made a contented smacking noise. "That hit the spot. Thank you."

She blushed despite herself. "You're welcome."

"So, do you already have the paint picked out, or do we still need to get some?" he asked before taking another long chug of sweet tea.

Abigail held her glass with both hands. The coolness felt nice even though the outdoors were still more than chilly enough. "I was thinking blue," she said, trying to picture the room after its forthcoming makeover. "It may be cliché, but it's also tried and true when it comes to baby boys. I haven't picked any up from the store yet, though."

"No worries," he told her without hesitation. "I can swing by after this."

"Why are you doing all this for me?" She took a measured sip to hide—and cool—the heat rising to her cheeks.

"I already said because you shouldn't be handling it in your condition, and because I care about you. It's what friends do. They show up and put up." He flashed her a debonair smile, but it didn't distract Abigail from the fact that her platonic male friend was the one who needed to help prepare for little

Owen's arrival, and that was because her husband was sadly no longer in the picture.

At least Gavin had better endurance and a stronger back than her father. She'd give him that.

"If you're sure," she said before hiding her face behind her glass again.

"I'm sure." His hair fell onto his forehead from the force of his nod, and she realized she liked it that way—a little messy from an honest afternoon's work.

Abigail watched Gavin disassemble the bed frame with a screwdriver he just happened to have in his pocket. *Men.*

"So what's the deal?" she asked, suddenly remembering that he had come baring multiple gifts and promises.

"Not yet. We have to finish in here first."

"Finish as in build the crib, or finish as in polish off the entire nursery?"

"The second one," Gavin said with a grunt as he dislodged a metal beam from the side of the bed. "That'll give you something to look forward to."

Abigail could have argued, but she rather liked the idea of knowing something pleasant was coming in her near future. Despite all the years that had passed since their initial friendship, she trusted him to take care of her, not disappoint her.

And even though he had shown up at her house to take care of all manner of husbandly tasks, that awkward tension hadn't lasted long. It was easy to fall in step beside him, regardless of what his feelings might or might not mean for them in the future.

"Hey, Gavin," she said after a spell. "Remember that time some butthead kid drove straight into the school?"

He popped his head up and groaned. "Please don't tell me that's the only memory you have of us together."

Abigail raised a finger to her chin and pretended to think about that rather than provide the answer she knew he wanted to hear too quickly. "I remember lots of things about us," she said at last to put him out of his misery.

"Oh, yeah? Then prove it." He set his screwdriver down, shifted himself away from the bed, and placed his chin on his hands in a dramatic display of anticipation. "Tell me five memories. Your five favorite."

"No pressure, right?" She laughed. What a production this was getting to be.

"There's never any pressure," he assured her, "but I do like revisiting the bygone days."

She thought about sitting down beside them, but these days getting up easily wasn't always a guarantee, and she'd rather not struggle like that in front of Gavin. "Well, one of my absolute favorites is when we had lunch together at Poogan's Porch and you opened up to me." She leaned back against the wall and turned her face to him.

"That one just happened. Can it really qualify as a memory?"

"Well, *I* remember it fondly," she countered with a giggle.

"Okay. What else?" He ran a hand through his sandy hair, messing it up even more than before.

"Definitely the time you drove into the school." When she saw that Gavin was about to protest, Abigail hurried along with a second, less embarrassing memory. "Then there was the time you surprised me at my locker and asked me to the homecoming dance. The dance itself was amazing."

"Yeah, those are all—for the most part—good, but you have one more."

"Right now," she admitted. "Right here in this exact moment. I already know it's going to be one of my favorites."

CHAPTER 30

PASTOR ADAM

Okay, so here's the truth. I did not have a meeting that afternoon. But because I couldn't bear to lie to my daughter, I set one up on the fly. Luckily, this sweet young couple I'd been counseling was all too happy to stop by my office for a chat about their upcoming nuptials.

I figured the Lord would forgive me this teeny fib since I'd done my best to make right on it. Also, I assure you, I'd misled my daughter with only the purest of intentions.

Even if Abigail didn't see how much she opened herself back up to the world from the very moment Gavin Holbrook stepped back into our lives, it certainly didn't escape my notice. One moment she would barely talk to me, and the next she was smiling again. Laughing even.

Oh, the church dogs definitely played their part, but something about that young man reached my baby girl's heart in a way that I just couldn't. I'd seen it back when they were kids, too. That's why I'd threatened to shoot him. It's a father's duty to protect his girl from getting her heart broken—especially when it looks like her heart is already halfway out the door to its new home.

Even now, even still, the life came back into her whenever Dr. Holbrook came around. So was it really all that wrong for me to try to help nudge them together?

Mind you, I prayed about it for a long time before my loving meddling began, and, yes, my plan is one-hundred percent God approved.

Now it was up to Abigail.

Of course, I was beside myself with joy when I returned home to find his truck parked outside, even though that meant I had to park at the curb myself. Inside, I found a storm of fluff roaring through the living room as the wide-eyed puppies chased each other's tails and competed for top spot in their little family pack. If you ask me, I think Brownie was ahead of the others by at least a few hard-earned points.

"Dad," Abigail said, appearing in the hall. "How was your meeting?"

"Good, good." I bobbed my head heartily in case she needed extra convincing. Then as casual as I could muster, I asked, "Was that Gavin's truck I saw out front?"

Her cheeks turned pink at the mention of that boy's name, and it didn't stop there. I swear to you, her forehead also blushed!

"Oh, yeah. He just stopped by to help with the nursery," she explained.

"That's nice of him," I said.

"Yeah." She smiled, and her pink skin darkened into a rich mulberry.

"Is he around? I'd like to say hello."

Abigail stepped aside and pointed back toward her old bedroom, then we both walked in to find Gavin wearing only jeans and a few odd splatters of paint as he dragged the roller back and forth across the walls, transforming the long-since faded pink into a vivid blue.

I cleared my throat.

"Hello, Pastor Elliott," the young man said before

using the back of his arm to wipe the sweat from his brow. He'd clearly been working hard, but...

"Don't you think you might want to keep your shirt on in mixed company?" I pressed. His button up lay discarded in the corner of the room, and I rushed to retrieve it for him.

Abigail kept her eyes on me—too embarrassed, I suppose, to make eyes at the fella in my presence. "I haven't been in here, Dad. Gavin said the fumes are bad for me and the baby, so I've been shut in my room reading while he works in here."

Good man, I thought. *Thank you for respecting and protecting my daughter and grandson.*

"Yeah, and you shouldn't really be here now." Gavin set his roller back in the tray and shrugged into the shirt I'd just handed him. "Why don't we all go to the living room where there aren't any harmful chemicals floating in the air?"

"Hey, baby girl," I coaxed. "You should really listen to him. He is a doctor, after all."

"I'm going!" Abigail shouted, raising both arms above her head in surrender as she turned back to the hall.

When she'd gone, I closed the door up tight. "Got a second brush?" I asked and waited for Gavin to provide it.

We painted together in silence for a few moments until I finally decided to come right out with it. "What are your intentions with my daughter?" I demanded.

He startled, and a few drops of blue fell onto the tarp below. "I believe you asked me that before, sir, and my answer hasn't changed."

"Which is?" I pressed, not because I didn't remember but because I wanted to see if he had.

"To make her happy," he said matter-of-factly.

"Any funny business this time?"

"Not unless she'll first accept my grandmama's ring," he answered, surprising us both with the intensity of his confession.

"Good answer. Good man." I tossed my paintbrush aside and wrapped him in a hug.

There it was, my proof that our plans were aligned. God was on our side, too. Now all we needed was a measure of time and a bit of bravery from our dear Abigail.

CHAPTER 31

ABIGAIL

When Abigail arrived at the Eternal Grace Church for her father's service the following Sunday, she was surprised to find Gavin waiting for her just as he had the week before.

"How'd you know I would be here?" she pressed, giving him a hug hello even though the two of them had worked together on the nursery the previous evening.

Gavin shrugged before bursting into his signature goofball grin. "Lucky guess, but I figured you'd come since your little one enjoys it so much," he pointed out, bringing back that perfect memory of her baby's first kick.

"That he does," she answered, giving him a

playful jab as they walked side by side into the sanctuary. "And now that he's started kicking me, he just won't stop. It's like he constantly wants to remind me that he's in there and that he'd like a bit more space, please and thank you."

"Smart guy. If I were him, I'd be doing whatever it takes to get your attention, too." He waited for Abigail to select their seats before plopping down beside her.

"Speaking of which," he continued as if there'd been no pause in the conversation at all. "I have a proposition for you both. Would the two of you like to accompany me on a picnic lunch after the service?"

"I don't know," Abigail teased, reaching both hands down to rest on her growing belly. "What do you think, little guy?"

"He says yes," Gavin quickly supplied.

She laughed, eliciting questioning glances from the family in the row behind them. "Do you two have a telepathic connection that I don't know about?"

"Nothing like that." He leaned in close and whispered to her, making their conversation private once again. "But I do know he likes it when you're happy, and trust me, this will make you both very happy."

"Do I finally get to hear your deal? Because the fact that you haven't told me yet is making me nuts!"

"Maybe," he said with a disarming smile that contradicted his noncommittal response.

Before Abigail could ask any more questions, the band started up. This marked the beginning of praise and worship and the end of their conversation...

For now.

After the service, Gavin begged and pleaded until Abigail at last agreed to let him drive to their secret picnic destination. Thankfully, he did not crash his truck into their old high school—or anything else, for that matter.

But he did drive a little faster than Abigail was normally comfortable with. "What's the hurry?" she wanted to know.

"Just excited to take you to one of my favorite places," he admitted, rolling down both windows and letting a cool breeze sweep through the truck's cab.

The crisp winter air blew Abigail's hair across her face, and it landed in her mouth whenever she tried to talk, but she didn't care.

"Are we going to the Angel Oak?" she asked, recognizing the path they were taking despite not having been out this way for longer than she cared to admit.

Gavin gasped, but still seemed please. "How'd you know?"

"Lucky guess," she teased, mimicking their conversation from earlier that morning. "I'm glad I'm right, though. I haven't been to the park over there since high school."

"That's way too long. I go at least once a season. Sometimes more."

"I've never seen it without its leaves," she admitted. "Do people still go year round?"

"I do. It's different each time," he said, pulling to a stop at the traffic light and turning to Abigail with utter joy written across his face. "Oh, but I wish you could've seen it on Christmas Eve when it was covered with snow. That's gotta be a once in a lifetime spectacle. But you know what? Sometimes lightning strikes twice, and that doesn't make the second time any less special."

Abigail stayed silent. It didn't seem like he was just talking about the tree, and she wasn't comfortable discussing a relationship yet.

"So, are you on team five hundred or fifteen hundred?"

She blinked over at him, completely lost. "What?"

"The Angel Oak," Gavin explained patiently. "How old do you think it is?"

Abigail thought back to what she'd learned about the tree. Not only was it the oldest living thing in Charleston, but some said it was the oldest thing in the United States period. She'd never thought much about it, always just considering the tree "really, really old." Both five hundred and fifteen hundred seemed impossibly large, and neither figure changed the majesty of that sprawling tree that sat alone, an island calling people from all over the world to come visit it.

"Five hundred, I guess," she said after considering it for a moment. "I'm practical like that. How about you?"

He laughed as he pressed down on the accelerator and jolted the truck back to life. "Definitely fifteen hundred."

"Why?"

He turned to her momentarily as he unleashed that favorite grin of hers. "Because I like believing in magic." His eyes were back on the busy Sunday traffic once more.

"Substitute miracles for magic, and you sound just like my father," she teased. Still, she wished she could believe like she used to. Would the old Abigail have chosen the magical response to Gavin's question instead of the practical one?

"He's not the worst person to sound like, I suppose." He pulled into the parking lot that serviced the Angel Oak park and began to search for a spot closest to the entrance. When at last he found one and cut the ignition, he turned toward Abigail and said, "He loves you like crazy, you know."

She nodded. "I know."

And so do you, she thought. Because the fact that Gavin wanted her was definitely insane. Couldn't he see that she wasn't going to be ready for a long time—if ever? Why not move on to somebody else?

CHAPTER 32

ABIGAIL

The Angel Oak was a true Lowcountry treasure. People came from all over the world to see it, but as is often the case when a treasure lies buried in your own backyard, Abigail hadn't paid it a second thought until Gavin brought her today.

The massive tree stretched clear up to the sky and in every direction besides. Some said it looked creepy with all those heavy, tangled branches reaching every which way, but Abigail liked to stick with the angel metaphor. Though if memory served, the name "Angel" came from the original owners of this land and not the heavenly host of beings.

"It's like this one tree is trying to hug the whole

world," she murmured in awe as they walked a slow circle around its trunk. "Or at least all of Charleston."

Gavin nodded and put an arm around her shoulder. "I feel connected here. To the past, present, and people who are too far out of my reach."

"Like to Susie and Millie?" Abigail asked, remembering the sorrow that had reflected in his eyes when she told him his story of love—of a family—lost.

"Yes," he said, his face remaining neutral for once as they continued their walk. "The last several times I've come out, it's been for them."

He stopped and turned toward Abigail, then grabbed both of her hands and swung them loosely between their bodies. "This time I'm here for you, though. Actually, both of us. We're here for us."

"What do you mean?" she asked. Fear filled her chest. Surely he meant to discuss their romantic feelings and possibilities again when she still wasn't anywhere near ready.

He looked up toward the top of the tree, which they couldn't see from where they were standing. It appeared as if the Angel Oak ascended forever into the heavens.

"For the sake of argument, let's say this tree is actually fifteen hundred years old," Gavin said before lowering his gaze to look at Abigail once more. "If you round our ages up to thirty, this tree has still lived fifty times longer than either of us. It makes us seem so short-lived by comparison. Doesn't it?"

"You sound like my father again," she teased in an effort to lighten the air of seriousness that now hung between them. "I'm sure he's used this argument in one of his sermons about Methuselah."

"I sound like me," he said without the slightest bit of humor. "This is all of me talking to all of you in front of all of this." He motioned widely at the tree.

"I'm sorry. I didn't mean to interrupt," Abigail whispered. "The tree does make me feel small. In size, too."

"Small, but not unimportant," he corrected. "More like there are things that are bigger than us out there. There are things that are bigger than us right here."

She nodded, unsure of where he was going with this.

"Now assuming we're still thirty, think about what one day of your life so far represents. You've lived over ten thousand days and still have many more to go. What I'm asking for is three hundred and fifty of them."

Nearly a year. What could he possibly want with that? She didn't follow. "I don't understand…"

"Abigail, I love you," he said bluntly but made no effort to kiss or embrace her. "I don't think I ever stopped."

She hung her head. Why had he trapped her here for this? She didn't want to hurt him, but she had nothing she could give, either.

Not yet.

Gavin continued, "But we both need time to heal, to rebuild our friendship. That's why I'd like to offer you a deal. We ran into each other again, after all those years, on the day after Christmas. I think—if you're willing—we should take any talk of a relationship off the table for one whole year. Until next year on that same day. Let's focus on being there for each other as friends, on helping each other heal. Then on the day after Christmas, we can meet here at the Angel Oak again and decide once and for all what we mean to each other. It's just one year—a little less—but I think it will go a long way to healing us both."

He hesitated before grabbing her wrist and directing her eyes toward his. "What do you think?"

A million questions shone in his eyes, but only one that mattered. *If you don't love me today, do you think you might tomorrow? Do you think you can love me within a year?*

The idea of delaying that conversation for a full year both terrified her—because that would mean that it was still coming—and relieved her. Now she just had to decide which reaction was stronger, and whether she'd be willing to give his plan a try.

CHAPTER 33

ABIGAIL

As silly as it seemed at first, taking the prospect of a relationship off the table for one full year was just what Abigail needed to get past her hang-ups about spending time with Gavin. Over the weeks that followed, their friendship grew.

And so did the puppies.

Now their ears stood straight up like true Chihuahuas, and those huge ears combined with those tiny bodies made them that much cuter. Abigail still favored Mama Mary most of all, but as it turned out, she had room in her heart—and during her days—for each and every one of those pups.

Most nights, Gavin joined Abigail and her father

for dinner at the kitchen table. They shared about their days, laughed, talked, and sometimes even caught a movie at the local cineplex.

Each morning, Gavin would text Abigail a status update about her baby. Every day brought a new fact about little Owen's development and about pregnancy and childbirth practices around the world. At twenty five weeks, her son was apparently the size of a rutabaga—though he was starting to look like an actual infant and even growing hair. She marveled at the changes happening inside her body. An entire life was growing inside of her. It wouldn't be long until little Owen was his own person, and that revelation shocked and amazed her each and every day.

On Valentine's Day, Gavin showed up with tacos—Abigail's number one pregnancy craving as of late—and a gift for her father, of all people. "First, we eat, then we have to take a little trip," he told them with a smile so big it spread around the entire room. Abigail guessed her baby might also be smiling in her womb, such was the infectiousness of Gavin with a surprise.

"What are we doing here?" her father remarked when Gavin drove them straight to the Eternal Grace Church and parked next to the two other cars in the lot that evening. "Not that I'd ever complain about the chance to spend time in God's house, mind you."

"You'll see," Gavin said, leading them toward the sanctuary.

Neither of the three ever missed a Sunday service now, but spending Valentine's Day with her father and with God… Well, that was a new one, all right.

The church secretary met them outside the double doors dressed in a becoming crushed velvet dress that graced her knees elegantly. Her hair was twisted into a neat and tidy updo, and her jewelry sparkled dazzlingly from her neck and earlobes.

"Mrs. Clementine, shouldn't you be out celebrating the holiday with your husband?" Abigail exclaimed upon seeing her there.

The old woman smiled but continued to block their entry. "That's where I'm heading next, but first, I wanted to be here for the look on your pa's face when—"

"Don't you dare, Mrs. Clementine," Gavin hissed. "We haven't managed to keep it a surprise for this long, only to spoil it at the last second!"

She slapped a manicured hand on her forehead. "Of course, you're right. You're right. C'mon inside, y'all. You're going to want to see this with your own eyes."

Abigail noticed the new addition to their sanctuary even before her father did. She gasped as she took in two large projector screens on either side of the church. Glancing toward the ceiling she, sure enough, saw a pair of projectors shooting colored beams at both.

Behind them, Gavin flipped off the light switches and the image on the screen became clear as day.

For all you do for others. Happy Valentine's Day, Pastor Adam! it said in white letters on a red background. Beneath that there was a very recent picture of Mama Mary and her pups posed in front of their locally famous nativity scene which had been put into storage weeks ago.

"How did you manage to do all this without either of us catching on?" Abigail asked with a stern look to Gavin while her father marched straight up to each projector and reached a trembling hand out toward the light.

"I have my ways," was the only answer Gavin would give. "Happy Valentine's Day, Abigail."

Her father returned and grabbed Gavin in a huge hug. He pulled Abigail in, too. "This is amazing. Thank you for giving the church such a wonderful gift. It will be much easier for everyone to read the words to our hymns now."

Mrs. Clementine spoke up for the first time since they'd entered the sanctuary. "It's not just for little old ladies with bad eyesight like me," she pointed out. "We can make slides to go along with your sermons and put them on the new church website for people to reference later—or to read for the first time in cases where they're too sick to attend in person."

"Can our church website do that?" her father asked in shock. "As far as I knew all it had was a few pictures, service times, and our address."

"It may need an update," Mrs. Clementine confessed, still wearing a broad smile. "But it will be very much appreciated by the congregation."

"You know," Gavin said, "with all the slides that will need to be put together each week plus the need for a new website, Eternal Grace may want to look to bringing a graphic designer on staff part-time. Now, where can we find one of those?"

Abigail's jaw dropped open. Of course. It was the perfect opportunity for her to stay busy and keep her skills up to date without putting too much pressure on her schedule as a soon-to-be mom. Gavin had done this for her father and for the church, but really, he had done it for her.

"I think that sounds like a mighty fine idea," her

father said, placing an arm over her shoulder. "Mighty fine, indeed."

And that's the exact story of how Abigail finally returned to work in the wake of her loss. It was a good story, and one she knew she would revisit often. It was amazing what good friends, good family, and a good God could accomplish.

CHAPTER 34

ABIGAIL

The new job at church helped Abigail to fill her days more efficiently. It also energized her like she hadn't been in months. Rather than sleeping her days away, she spent her free time reading up on some of the best nationally recognized therapy dog programs and all the other great working roles dogs could fill in society.

It was one thing for her father to claim their church dogs were miraculous, and quite another to intentionally set them up to help change people's lives. True, most working dogs belonged to much larger breeds, but while it wasn't common for Chihuahuas to have jobs, it absolutely could be done.

There were so many different types of therapy dogs, it made her head spin. Ultimately, Abigail decided it would be best to teach their church dogs how to help people going through difficult life transitions and battling with depression. After all, Mama Mary had helped her with just that thing. And while she wasn't fully recovered, she was making progress every day. Sometimes just having a nonjudgmental ear and a friendly lick could work wonders.

When Abigail shared her intention to get Mary and her pups certified as therapy dogs, her father ate the idea right up. "Ahh, perfect. That's just what our church needs. I told you God had a plan."

She laughed, all the while appreciating what her father's faith coupled with her research could accomplish.

By the time she reached twenty-eight weeks pregnant, the puppies had all turned eight weeks old, which meant they were ready to be enrolled in obedience school. During the first class, three of four puppies piddled on the floor of the gymnasium, and the fourth attacked and shredded a pamphlet about the importance of training dogs young. Still, Abigail was not discouraged.

"Well, we can only go up from here," she

confided in the pups while loading them back into the car to head home. "Maybe one of you will earn the title of 'most improved pup.' At least we can hope."

A sleek black SUV she didn't recognize was waiting for her in the driveway when she and the puppies returned. Abigail peeked inside, but the car sat empty. Hesitantly, she pushed the front door open and was greeted by her mother-in-law, who she hadn't seen since the day of Owen's funeral.

"Hello," Abigail said with a shaky voice, picking up Mama Mary who had run to greet her at the door and hugging the dog close. "It's nice to see you… Mom."

She'd always felt strange calling Owen's mother "Mom," but it had made him happy, which is why she did it anyway.

The older woman was tall and thin, with bright red hair and age spots where freckles had once been. Abigail had always liked her well enough, but it was hard for the two of them to spend time together after Owen had died.

They shared too many sad memories.

Mrs. Sutton approached her with tears in her eyes. "May I?" she asked, motioning toward Abigail's protruding belly.

Abigail nodded, and her mother-in-law placed a hand on each side of her belly. "Oh!" she cried. "He kicked me."

"He does that a lot," Abigail said. "I'm going to name him Owen, by the way."

Tears fell in earnest now, and Mrs. Sutton's face turned the same shade of burgundy as her hair. "That's a wonderful name. He would be so proud."

"I like to think he *is* proud," Abigail said gently. "That he's in Heaven experiencing every moment with us." Her faith had grown tremendously since her visit with Gavin to the Angel Oak. The faith she'd once resisted had brought her the beginnings of peace that she'd so desperately craved since her husband's passing.

"That's a nice thought, dear." Owen's mother smiled sadly.

"I didn't mean to cut you out of things," Abigail explained. "It's been hard, and I—"

"No need to apologize. I wasn't ready to see you yet, either," the mother confessed as she tightened a hand around the strap of her purse. "The only thing harder than losing your spouse, they say, is losing a child."

Abigail's heart ached for them both. "When the baby's born, I want you to be a part of his life. Same as you would be if Owen were still here. Family is too important to keep little Owen away from any of the people who love him."

"Thank you," Mrs. Sutton said. "I want to be there for him, and for you. It's just…" Her words trailed away as if they were still too painful to speak.

"*Hard,* I know," Abigail finished for her. "Believe me, I know."

"Actually, I don't think they've made a word strong enough for it yet." Mom let out a sad chuckle. "I finally got the courage to sort through all of Owen's old things. There were boxes upon boxes in the attic, in his old bedroom. There was so much, yet it didn't feel like enough to represent a whole life. Not even close."

Abigail nodded and listened, waiting for Mrs. Sutton to say more.

"I couldn't part with anything. Not yet," Owen's mother continued. "It felt wrong to simply give it all away to people who didn't know him and wouldn't value any of the things that had once been so important

"And so…" She sniffed and wiped away tears before continuing. "I'm starting small by bringing some of these memories to you, so you can share them with Owen's son. I know you will both treasure them like I would, and that makes it a little bit easier. I packed a box for you. It's in my trunk."

"Thank you, Mom. I'd love to have it." Abigail wasn't sure what to do next. Should she hug Mrs. Sutton? Offer to retrieve the box from her car? Instead, she asked the easiest of the many questions on her mind. "Where's my dad?"

Mrs. Sutton gave her a sad smile. "He let me in, then went for a drive. Said we'd need time alone together before he was there to get in the way."

Yes, that sounded just like her dad, although it may have been easier if he was here to mediate for them.

The two women stood in awkward silence for a moment.

"Oh, let me go get the box for you," Owen's mother said after reaching in her purse for a crumpled tissue.

Abigail waited inside, both terrified and eager for what she might find.

If only she knew…

CHAPTER 35

PASTOR ADAM

Things in our little corner of the world had been going peachy keen for more than a month now. Thanks to Gavin's generous donation to the church, our little congregation welcomed in many new families who appreciated Eternal Grace's blend of modern technology mixed with classic praise and worship.

I swear to you, that boy was a genius. I'm really quite glad I didn't shoot him back in the day.

Best of all, Abigail stayed busy and happy with her new role at the church along with starting things up for the Chihuahuas and their career ambitions as therapy dogs. Yes, Abigail was happy as a clam…

Until one day she wasn't.

Oh, I knew trouble was coming when Mrs.

Sutton showed up at our house. Not that she would do anything to hurt my Abigail. She was a decent enough woman, but pain seemed to be contagious around here lately.

And wouldn't you know it? I returned home from my drive about to find Mrs. Sutton's car gone and my daughter lying in tears on the living room floor. The puppies, whose bed had been moved out of Abigail's room and into the living room, all eagerly lapped at her tears while Mama Mary remained nestled into her side, trying to offer comfort via warmth. A sizable cardboard box sat atop the table, its scattered contents covering the surface.

"Baby girl, *honey,*" I whispered, coming as close as the puppies would allow. "What happened?"

She looked up at me with scratchy red eyes and a face to match. I'd only been gone for about an hour, but apparently the damage had been more than done.

"I can't talk about it right now," she told me. "I thought I was getting better, but this... this is too much." Her eyes guided me to the box that sat open on the table, inviting me to take a look and see for myself.

As hard as it was to turn away and leave Abigail to her sorrow, I needed to know what had upset her so greatly. Inside that box and all around it were mementos, tokens from Owen's life—an old high school letter jacket, a worn teddy bear, dozens of photo albums including several pictures that appeared to have been printed directly off of Facebook or some such site, and even an old baby book.

"It was nice of her to bring these by," I said with caution.

"Was it?" Abigail asked me with a cracked voice.

"Memories are worth cherishing," I answered, knowing full well that one day she'd be glad to have these things to look back on with her son.

"Memories hurt," she said, stroking Mama Mary's soft fur. "This hurts."

I placed the items back into the box and carried it to my bedroom, the one spot in the house where my daughter was least likely to come across it by accident.

"When you're ready for it," I told her upon returning, "all you have to do is ask."

"That's the thing," she said, her voice still shaky. "What if I'm never ready?"

"Then that's just fine, baby girl," I said, lowering myself to the floor even though it meant pushing several puppies out of my way in the process. "That's just fine."

CHAPTER 36

ABIGAIL

Abigail's father left her to her tears but remained nearby as she struggled through the flood of emotions that had hit her that day. She'd finally begun to look toward the future, toward her son and the life they would lead together, to the possibility of one day allowing herself to fall in love again.

But that box from Owen's mother was perfect proof that when you fell, you got hurt. She'd loved her husband with everything she had. They had built a life to live together, until suddenly it collapsed and Abigail found herself back home with her father.

So much optimism they'd had when decorating their home, arguing over whose family traditions they'd honor for each holiday, planning the perfect wedding and then seeing it through. They'd never expected for it to come crashing down all around them—that one of them wouldn't make it out of the mess alive.

Or that it would practically kill her, too.

Thanks to her father, the dogs, and—yes—Gavin, she'd been able to start rebuilding, but as it turned out, she was the little piggy who'd built her house from straw. One blow and everything came tumbling down around her.

She'd always been the sentimental type, or at least since her mother had disappeared and left her behind. Her way of moving on had apparently been not to think about Owen. One medium-sized box ended up being a giant trigger. Everything rushed back, the pain fresh and new and not patched up as she had started to believe.

Abigail knew she needed to be stronger. In fact, she didn't have a choice. Her son would arrive in about three months, and he'd depend on her for everything. If she couldn't even take care of herself, how could she care for a newborn baby?

It terrified her, the thought of failing her son—of failing Owen's son, his one living legacy. That she could be triggered by anything and at any moment meant that nothing was fully safe, no day guaranteed.

The most frightening thing of all, though, was that she had almost allowed it to happen again. Her friendship with Gavin had become vital to her these past few months. The more time that passed, the more she thought that—yes—she could really love him. She could really build a new life and future.

He'd once told her that sometimes lightning struck twice and that each time was equally special. The truth of the matter was that lightning strikes were terrible, painful disasters. She'd somehow managed to survive her first but wouldn't be strong enough if the lightning found her again.

One can recover from pain if the pain stops, but what if a fresh blaze destroyed everything that's left? She'd loved and lost Owen. Could she handle loving Gavin when there was always—always—the possibility she could lose him as well? She never thought her husband dying would happen, but it had.

Gavin could fall out of love with her, find someone else, change… he could die, too.

What was she thinking? It was already scary enough to have a baby on the way. It would take everything she had to keep him safe and raise him well. She didn't have anything to risk, couldn't possibly stand losing anything more. Because if she did, she wouldn't be able to nurture and provide for her son like he needed and deserved.

Sometimes you had to make sacrifices for the greater good. As horrible as it was to think about, that's exactly what Owen had done. He'd given his life for his country. Now Abigail would give her last chance at love for her son.

Things with Gavin needed to end. Even though he'd taken a relationship off the table until the day after Christmas, both of their feelings continued to stretch and grow. If she waited, he'd hurt that much more in the end.

Oh, she prayed he would know it wasn't his fault, that she didn't want to hurt him the way Susie had. But truth be told, she already had a family, too. And she owed it to them to protect her heart.

She was thinking about all this, determination growing within her, when Gavin arrived with an armful of knit baby blankets.

"My mother couldn't help herself," he said with a laugh before spying Abigail on the ground and her father at the table. "Oh no, what happened? Is the baby okay?"

"The baby's fine," she assured him, struggling to sit.

Gavin kneeled at her side to help her up.

How could she possibly begin the conversation they needed to have? She started weeping all over again. When would the tears stop? She'd shed so many tears this past year, she was practically a fountain of sorrow.

"What's wrong?" he coaxed gently.

Her father walked out of the room, and a moment later she heard his bedroom door latch shut behind him.

Gavin turned to her with a knitted brow and searching eyes, and Abigail said the only two words that pushed through into her brain.

"I can't."

Gavin forced a smile. It held none of the usual mirth or mischief. He already knew.

She didn't have to say more, but she owed it to him to try. "You've been such a good friend to me, but I don't think I can see you anymore."

His pain became visible on his face, in his posture. "Did I do something wrong?" he asked.

"No, you've been perfect," she said, crying and both wishing and not wishing that he would take her in his arms. "That's the problem."

"I pushed you too hard. It was too much, too fast." Gavin turned red as he searched for the reason why. But Abigail already knew he would never find it.

He couldn't understand not having experienced it for himself, and for that she was very grateful.

Abigail placed a gentle kiss on his cheek—a kiss goodbye. "You've been perfect, but I'll never even be close to that. I'm too broken already."

He grabbed both of her hands. "You're perfect to me. Abigail, I love you."

"I wish I could let myself love you, Gavin, but I need to give everything I have left to my son. You understand that, don't you?"

Gavin turned away from her so she couldn't see the pain that mangled his face. But she heard it all the same. "You know where to find me if that ever changes," he said. "Goodbye, Abigail."

CHAPTER 37

ABIGAIL

Abigail was relieved that Gavin didn't try to fight for her. She'd made up her mind, and he respected that now. She sorely missed all the time they had spent together—he'd been a great friend—but threw herself into work at the church and with the dogs as well as preparing for little Owen's arrival.

As the days became weeks which then became months, Abigail found this second sting of loss transformed into a dull, quiet ache. This time, it had been on her own terms and with her child's best interests at heart. Gavin was a good man, and she didn't doubt he would find somebody wonderful to share his life with, someone far better than the wreck Abigail had become.

Then one day, Abigail woke up with a cramping pain that just wouldn't quit. When it still hadn't abated by dinner, her father forced her into his car so that he could drive her to the hospital. She was still two weeks out from her due date and understood that most first babies arrived late. Little Owen, however, did not seem to understand this, because less than twenty-four hours later, her beautiful baby boy joined her in that hospital room.

Her father didn't leave her side for a single moment. When they called Owen's mother, she, too, tended to Abigail during the labor, creating a room full of love just as she'd hoped would be the case when welcoming her child into the world.

A flurry of folks from the church paraded in and out of the maternity ward, bringing their well wishes along with flowers for Abigail, gifts for the baby, and of course casseroles for her father. She wondered if Gavin had heard the news and if he would try to stop by and offer his congratulations. It felt odd not having him here when he had been so involved in preparing the nursery and had even gifted them the blanket that little Owen was swaddled in that day.

Looking into her son's perfect face now, though, she knew she would do anything to protect him for as long as she lived. Her life was no longer her own, and that was perfectly fine by Abigail.

When she awoke from a brief nap the next morning, she found a most unusual gift sitting on the window pane. While others brought more traditional flowers like daisies, daffodils, and tulips, this plant was all green. Upon closer inspection, she saw that it was a bonsai tree whose limbs had been twisted and shaped to resemble the far-reaching arms of the Angel Oak on John's Island. There was only one person that gift could be from, although the little tree arrived with no note attached.

She was glad to see that Gavin was still thinking of her fondly and hoped the absence of a note meant he had moved past the hurt she had burdened him with.

When little Owen stirred, she got up from the hospital bed. Her stitches still stung, but she felt freer than she had in months as she padded over to cuddle her child.

"Look at this, little man," she said, rocking him gently in her arms as they both approached the window. She knew he couldn't see far yet, but he loved listening to her voice, which meant she talked to him as much as she could think to say.

"This little tree represents a much bigger, older

tree. In fact, we have our own special bit of magic right here in Charleston. One day when you're older, I'll take you to see it," she promised.

"Oh, good you're up!" her father said, pacing into the room as he clutched at his belly. "If I eat one more helping of casserole, I think the good Lord might call me home."

Abigail laughed. "Your grandpa is such a silly old man," she told her son, who had reached one hand out of his blanket and was stretching it toward her. "We're going to have to tell all the church ladies to stop feeding him so well."

"I'll hold you to that," her father said. "As it turns out, I just can't say no to a good plate of home cooking, but that's not why I'm happy to see you up."

"Oh?" Abigail lifted her son higher in her arms and kissed his fuzzy little head.

"I used my Godly connections to accomplish a little favor from the hospital staff, and well… bring her in, Mrs. Clementine."

And sure as day, Mama Mary trotted into the room like she owned the place. She even wore a tiny hospital gown and plastic booties on her feet. The moment she saw Abigail, she broke into a run, pulling her leash clean out of Mrs. Clementine's hand.

"Oh, Mary! Look, we're both mamas now!" Abigail cried, happy to see her best canine friend.

Mary barked happily, but Abigail shushed her. "Not now. You only just got here, and I don't want them to take you away before you have a chance to meet my little one. Would you help us out, Dad?"

Abigail settled back onto the bed with Owen in her arms, and her father came to sit beside her holding on to the sweet mother Chihuahua so she could say hello.

Mrs. Clementine snapped a picture and gushed, "How nice! The whole family's here!"

"Well, not the whole family," her father said.

Abigail opened her mouth to correct him. Gavin wasn't part of the family, not anymore, and it wasn't very nice of him to remind her of that on what should be a happy day.

Before she could say anything, though, her father continued, "We'll have to wait until we're at home to introduce Muffin, Cupcake, Cookie, and Brownie. They're probably still a mite too hyper to be around little Owen."

Abigail laughed and nodded, posed for another picture, then looked toward the bonsai replica of the Angel Oak. She had everything now, so why did she still miss Gavin?

Little Owen's face scrunched up, and he let out a goat-like cry.

"Oops, didn't know we were intruding on breakfast time," her father said, leading Mrs. Clementine and Mama Mary from the room. "We'll just wait outside until you're through."

Abigail listened for the click of the door behind them before fitting her son to her breast. As she watched him nurse, she remembered the reasons behind her decision to end her friendship with Gavin.

She needed to be strong for her child, and she needed to stay that way, too.

No matter what else happened.

CHAPTER 38

ABIGAIL

Abigail had always known that early motherhood would be a lot of hard work, but she was not prepared for the exhaustion that came with it. Whoever made the rule to sleep when the baby sleeps must have had a great little sleeper on her hands.

And although Owen wasn't terrible by any means, he would wake a few times each night to cry out for Abigail. This made it hard to track days. In a way, it had all been one very long day since he was born in May.

Her fatigue reached amazing new levels in early December when Owen began to crawl. He and the puppies, who were almost full grown now but just as feisty and playful as ever, could cause mischief together. And, oh, did they ever!

The worst of it happened a few days before Christmas when the cyclone of fur knocked their evergreen tree clear over. Luckily, little Owen wasn't involved in that particular fiasco, but he did pull a platter of cookies off of the end table when Abigail was distracted in cleaning up the mess of scattered ornaments and tinsel that the Chihuahuas had left in their wake.

"Your Christmas present is extra obedience classes," she told them while wagging her finger.

They all sat in a line and looked up at her with tails wagging merrily as if to show they were already the perfect little angels.

Mama Mary groaned and went to hide under Abigail's favorite chair, but not before first swiping a fallen cookie.

"That's not good for you!" Abigail cried, but now Owen had a cookie, too, which meant she had to choose which battle she preferred to fight that day.

"Ah-ha, gotcha!" she swiped the broken gingerbread man from Owen, who then began to cry. "Where are you, Dad?" Abigail moaned.

Of course, by the time he returned half an hour later, both puppies and human child had begun their afternoon naps, leaving the house serene and peaceful and nothing like it had been less than an hour ago.

"Looks like y'all had a nice day," her father said with a proud grin.

She simply laughed and swiped the tray of recovered cookies away from him before he could steal one for himself. "I wouldn't eat those if I were you."

"Do I want to know?" he asked with raised brows.

Abigail just shook her head and walked away. It was a chaotic life, but a blessed one.

The following day was Christmas Eve. This time Abigail not only attended the service, but helped to lead it. Even Mama Mary and her pups made an appearance. Thankfully, Mrs. Clementine was all too happy to look after little Owen while his mother was busy with church duties. Abigail even made her an honorary grandmother, which meant she doted on Owen extra.

After church, they captured pictures of the Chihuahua family in that same locally famous nativity scene where they'd been born and first discovered.

"Happy Birthday, babies!" Abigail cried.

Owen clapped his pudgy hands with glee.

To think, just one year ago, Abigail had been all by herself. Her father had been there for her, but she'd shut him out. Everything had changed last Christmas with the discovery of those puppies, and now she and her father had Owen in their worlds, too.

Despite the added mischief, his childish antics were exactly what Abigail had needed to fill her days and her heart once more. It was hard to believe she'd ever doubted the love she would have for him. She enjoyed being a mother more than anything.

"It was a good day," her father said when they were back at home sitting before a roaring fire and noshing on a fresh batch of Christmas cookies. This time they had chocolate chip.

"It was," she agreed. "A long day."

"Merry Christmas, baby girl."

"Merry Christmas, Dad." Abigail closed her eyes and leaned back into the chair, enjoying the quiet comfort of the evening. She was surprised when her father spoke again.

"I know it somewhat breaks with tradition, but I was wondering if you might like to open your stocking tonight."

"That's okay, Dad," she answered with a satisfied sigh. "I don't mind waiting."

"Let me rephrase that. You should open your stocking tonight."

She opened her eyes and glanced at her father suspiciously. "Why?"

He winked at her in a move that was very St. Nick, especially given his ever growing bowl full of jelly. "Let's just say it has time sensitive material."

Abigail shrugged and went to retrieve her stocking from the mantle place. Immediately, she found that it was much lighter than it had been in years past. Reaching in, she found a single small item, which she wrapped her fingers around and pulled out.

It was a silver locket shaped like a heart. On the front were the initials RE.

"Was this Mom's?" she asked, feeling the weight of it in her palm.

His gaze softened. "Yes, I gave it to her the first Christmas after you were born. I figured this would be the perfect time to give it to you now that you're a mother yourself."

"Thank you, Dad," she said, practically short of breath from the sudden burst of excitement. "I love it."

"Open it," he prompted.

It took some doing since the necklace hadn't been worn in decades, but eventually Abigail was able to pry open the little heart. On one side she found a close up of her and Owen's faces on their wedding day, both very much in love and with no idea what the future would hold for them. The other side showed a candid shot of her and Gavin, heads leaned in close to each other as they both laughed over something she could no longer remember.

"What's this all about?" she asked, feeling hurt that her father would ruin this perfect gift by reminding her of both the men she had lost.

He took a deep breath before explaining. "Baby girl, as your father, it was my job to teach you faith, and I'm so proud of the strong Christian woman you've become. The next great man in your life, Owen, taught you love, and I will forever be thankful to him for that. But Gavin… Gavin taught you laughter when you needed it the most. Don't throw that away."

"You never moved on past Mom," she said, fully angry with him now. "How could you expect me to move on past Owen? That isn't fair."

"No," he said simply. "None of what's happened has been fair. The worst of it all is that you shut out someone who loves you just because you were scared."

"Of course I'm scared!" she shouted, praying the

baby wouldn't wake from her carelessness. "I lost everything."

"And how blessed you are to have found it again," her father said before pushing himself up from his seat and leaving her alone in the darkening living room.

CHAPTER 39

ABIGAIL

On Christmas day, Abigail, her father, and little Owen joined her in-laws to celebrate. They lived about two hours away, but Abigail vowed to make the journey upstate to visit at least once per month so that the new grandparents wouldn't miss out on getting to know their grandson.

By the time they returned to Charleston that evening, Abigail was utterly exhausted from their long day of festivities coupled with the four hours of driving. The following day was Sunday, which meant her father would be in for another long day. She didn't know if she could handle it herself, though—or if Owen could, for that matter.

She turned off her alarm and decided to leave it to

chance. By the time she awoke the following morning, her father had already left for first service. She was surprised that little Owen hadn't stirred and gently padded to his nursery, only to find her baby had been replaced by a single sheet of lined paper.

Abigail, it read in her father's jagged scrawl. I took Owen with me to church. Mrs. Clementine would have my neck if I denied her Sunday cuddles with him. I didn't want to wake you, but I did want to tell you to look in the top drawer of Owen's dresser. I know you'll make the right decision.

Love,

Dad

She clutched the note to her chest as she crossed the room to the honey oak dresser and pulled open the first drawer. In it lay her first Bible, the same one her father had regifted her last year. When she picked the tiny book up, her mother's locket fell onto the folded onesies below.

Why was he giving these to her now, and why had he brought them to Owen's room? She thought back to when she'd pulled the Bible from her stocking last year. He'd wanted to remind her of happier times and said that Owen wouldn't want her to wallow. This year, she'd found the locket tucked into the bottom of that same stocking, and he'd told her not to throw away her chance with Gavin.

But why was he harping on this? She'd found God again. She had a great job, a son whom she adored. She was happy again. The love she felt for her father, her son, her dogs, and her God had given her the strength she'd once lost. And now…

Oh, no.

Love wasn't weakness like she had allowed herself to believe. It wasn't something to be feared and sacrificing it wouldn't be doing her son any favors. Love was what had made her whole again. Love was what gave her strength, life.

And she'd thrown Gavin's love straight out the window, when it had been a big part of helping her to find a life worth living again. He'd given her all of himself, but she'd been stingy. Afraid. Unable.

What a terrible mistake she'd made.

She opened up the Bible and found a torn page from her father's page-a-day calendar. It talked about new hope, new chances, and on the center of the tiny sheet of paper, a giant 26 was written in big, bold strokes.

It was the day after Christmas, the same day she'd run into Gavin at the pet store last year, the same day they'd promised to meet under the Angel Oak and decide whether their relationship should go further. He'd asked her for one year, and she hadn't even given him that.

She didn't deserve for him to be waiting for her under that magical old tree, but she had to at least try. She had to go and see if he remembered, if he still wanted her despite all the hurt she had caused them both.

"C'mon, Mama Mary," she called, not caring that she was still dressed in her pajamas. She needed to get to John's Island and fast, and she needed the moral support that only her special little dog could provide.

"Please, God. Please don't let it be too late," she prayed during the entire drive over. Her mother's locket lay against her collarbone, and she lifted a hand to stroke it. Her mother had walked away from a good man, but Abigail would not repeat her mistakes, not if she could help it.

She parked and jumped out of the car, racing around to grab Mama Mary from the passenger's side. She caught a glimpse of herself in the side mirror and gasped. She looked a fright, but she didn't care. She'd let silly things, incorrect notions, rob her of her joy before, and she was done making the same mistakes over and over again.

She clipped Mama Mary into her leash and

walked toward the giant oak looming in the distance. Just as before, its branches reached out to hug all of Charleston. She squinted as she drew near, searching each face in the park.

And then she saw him.

"Gavin!" she cried, breaking into a full sprint with Mama Mary trailing behind. She let go of the leash so she could run faster, knowing her dog would follow along obediently.

He turned toward her, and that goofy grin she had missed so much lit his entire face. "You came!" he called to her, standing in place as she continued to run as fast as her legs would carry her.

"Gavin!" she cried again, reaching him at last and tackling him with a hug. And wouldn't you know it? There she was, crying again.

"You came," he repeated, brushing her messy hair away from her face.

"I finally realized a few things I should have known a long time ago," she said between pants for air.

"Such as?" he asked. It was then she noticed he was holding his breath. He still didn't know. He'd never known because she hadn't told him.

"That I love you. I want only you. Little Owen and I both need you in our lives."

"You love me?" he asked, his grin growing even wider than she'd once thought possible.

"So much," she whispered. "So much it hurts. I'm so sorry I sent you away. I was scared."

"I know." When he nodded his understanding, a fresh tear fell from his cheek and landed on Abigail's pajama shirt.

"I don't want to be scared anymore," she continued. "I want to be brave for you. For us. I love you so much, Gavin Holbrook."

"Are you done apologizing?" Gavin asked, raising his palm to stroke her cheek. "Because you have nothing to be sorry for. You're here now and that's more than I could have ever hoped for. I don't care about your past, Abigail Sutton-Elliott. I only want your future, and I hope that maybe one day you'd be willing to become Abigail Sutton-Elliot-Holbrook."

Before Abigail could ask whether Gavin was officially trying to propose to her, he brought his lips to hers in a delicate, inspiring, life-affirming kiss.

Sometimes love hurt.

Other times it healed, but always—always—it was a miracle.

CHAPTER 40

PASTOR ADAM

It may have taken a whole year, but finally my daughter found the gift waiting right in front of her. When I returned home from church that Sunday to find her and Gavin cuddled up together on my living room couch, I whooped so loud it made the puppies run in a barky blur searching the house for an intruder or some other such oddity that would explain my sudden outburst.

Gavin rose to meet me, extending his hand for a shake and taking a hug right along with it. "Thank you," he whispered into my ear. "Thank you for helping her see."

"I didn't do it for you," I said with a smile despite the harshness of my words. "I did it for my baby girl. I'd do anything for her."

Gavin laughed. "I remember the shotgun."

"There never was a shotgun," I admitted. "I just had to make sure you were good enough for my daughter."

"And what's the verdict?"

I hesitated to make him sweat a little before wrapping him in another hug, clapping him on the back, and saying, "Welcome to the family, son."

Of course, he's not an official part of the family yet, but Gavin's been one of us ever since he returned to our lives that fateful day after Christmas. It won't be long until things are official, though. The kids are planning their wedding for May at that very same oak tree that's become so important to them. I'll be officiating, and little Owen will serve as the best man and the ring bearer all in one.

Don't worry, the church dogs will be there with us, too. They wouldn't miss it for the world.

WHAT'S NEXT?

Some folks are born with a silver spoon jutting right out of their mouths. Others are a bit more like Miss Harmony King. That poor thing bounced in and out of so many foster homes growing up even my head spun circles trying to keep track of them all.

Once Harmony hit eighteen, though, she disappeared from Charleston altogether. Fast forward nearly a decade and now she's back, bent over a pew and praying like her life depends on it. I'd reckon that just maybe it does.

Of course, I don't know why this young woman left our town, and I don't know why she's come back now—but one thing I do know, beyond the shadow of a doubt, is that God meant for us to find each other again.

So I told Harmony the story of the special Chihuahuas born in our church's nativity scene last Christmas Eve, and that our Muffin, in particular, wanted to help her if she'd let him. Yes, these Little Loves have worked miracles before, and by the grace of the Almighty, I think they might just be about to perform another…

Get your copy at www.MelStorm.com/LittleLoves

AFTERWORD

It shouldn't be a surprise to learn that I am head over heels for the mighty little breed commonly known as *Chihuahua!*

It wasn't always that way, though. I, too, bought into the negative PR that called members of the tiniest dog breed vicious, crazed ankle biters with a Napoleon complex.

But then my little girl became utterly obsessed. She begged and pleaded for her own Chihuahua to love. Mind you, it took us several months to realize what she was begging for, as our then-three-year-old princess said she "needed a Jawa."

So, after several talks that always ended with, "Ugh, why a Chihuahua? I really don't want one of

AFTERWORD

those!" we finally took her to meet a litter of puppies. We reasoned she wouldn't actually want one of these tiny terrors once she met some in person.

But we were wrong again!

A couple weeks later, we brought home our first *Jawa*, which she proudly named "Sky Princess." Okay, fine. This was my daughter's dog, and she already loved it like crazy. We had four other awesome dogs and—seriously—how much trouble could a one pound puppy actually get into?

I was on a tight writing deadline at the time, so asked my husband to take care of the puppy during the day while our little girl was at school. He did, but occasionally the little pupster wanted to spend time with me in my office.

And she always—always!—begged for me to pick her up and set her on my desk. Once there, she'd cuddle into my chest and even climb into my shirt to snuggle. She was too little to climb the stairs by herself, so I took to carrying her up at night for bedtime.

Speaking of bedtime, the crafty little thing actually figured out how to open her crate and came to cry at our bedroom door during her second night with us.

AFTERWORD

Little by little, I fell in love... and, oh, I was a goner!

A few months later, we found out that Sky Princess's mother needed a new home due to sudden health issues with her original owner, and now I was the one begging and pleading: "Please give me my dog's mom!"

And so we welcomed our second Jawa to the fold, Mama Mila, who—you guessed it—was the basis for Mama Mary in this book. With two wonderful, loving cuddle bugs to call our own, I quickly moved from hate, to indifference, to like, to an overwhelming devotion to these little dogs—these mini miracles.

Did you know that Chihuahuas are the second most euthanized dog breed in America? It's sadly true. That's why I one day hope to open my own rescue and breed education program to show the world just how lucky we are to have Chihuahuas in it.

I never knew such a tiny dog could fill my heart so completely! Now imagine having two. Or, in the case of Abigail and Pastor Adam, five.

There are so many Jawas—so many dogs—out there who need a second chance at forever. Don't look past the Chihuahua just because you've heard some not-so-nice rumors. Each dog deserves to be judged for her own heart.

Each dog is a blessing.

And, yes, a miracle.

ACKNOWLEDGMENTS

I have wanted to write this book for such a long time. Once I fell in love with my own special Chihuahua girl, Sky Princess (and later her Mama Mila), I knew I needed to write a book series to celebrate them.

And, finally, here we are!

I always have so many people to thank, but I wanted to make this batch of acknowledgments special—so here we go, all the people who helped me make this book a reality, in chronological order of their contribution.

Thanks go to my family for encouraging my creativity and rarely saying no when I wanted yet another book to add to my massive home library.

To my husband, Falcon, for showing me what love was and that I was worthy of it. For taking care of things around the house so I can focus on writing, and for never failing to believe in me and encourage me to keep on going after my dreams. Just because you catch a dream doesn't mean you should ever stop chasing it, right?

To my daughter, Phoenix, for turning me into a certifiably crazy Chihuahua lady.

To my friend, Mina Jandou, for entrusting me first with Sky Princess and then Mama Mila. Thank you for bringing the magic of Chihuahuas into my life, thank you for loving them every bit as much as I do, and thank you for being your beautiful, wonderful self!

To my two Chihuahua girls for inspiring the series and lending such life-like qualities to Mama Mary and her puppies. To my non-Chi dogs as well, because I also love and am inspired by them.

To my cover designer, Mallory Rock, for bringing my vision to life with her art—and for suggesting that we use Sky Princess as one of the cover models!

To my fabulous assistant and friend, Angi Hegner. Thank you for getting excited about my books and forcing me to write them in a timely fashion, even though I definitely know I'm not easy to manage. And to Becky Muth and Shanae Johnson for also getting excited as my word count increased.

To Mallory Crowe for doing write-ins with me and just generally being awesome. You are thanked, my dear.

To my amazingly talented editor—and another of my many cheerleaders—Megan Harris. She's the real deal, folks, and my work is the better for it.

To my proofreader, Jasmine Bryner, who always gives such great feedback and insights while she's reading and lives the story right alongside me.

To my readers. To you. For letting my books into your heart and giving me a voice, for writing me such kind notes of encouragement, and for getting excited about the characters who are so near and dear to my heart.

And to anyone who's ever loved a Chihuahua, who's ever helped a dog in need, who's ever believed in miracles—no matter how small.

Thank you all. You are appreciated more than you know and loved more than you might expect!

GET TEXT UPDATES

Well, here's something cool… You can now sign up to get text notifications for all my most important book news. You can choose to receive them for New Releases, New Pre-Orders, or Special Sales--or any combination of the three.

These updates will be short, sweet, and to the point with a link to the new book or deal on your favorite retailer.

You choose when you receive them, making this new way of communicating fully customized to your needs as a reader.

Sign up at www.MelStorm.com/TextMe

MORE FROM MELISSA STORM

Sign up for free stories, fun updates, and uplifting messages from Melissa at www.MelStorm.com/gift

Sweet Promise Press

Saving Sarah

Flirting with the Fashionista

* * *

The Sled Dog Series

Get ready to fall in love with a special pack of working and retired sled dogs, each of whom change their new owners' lives for the better.

Let There Be Love

Let There Be Light

Let There Be Life

Season of Mercy

Season of Majesty

Season of Mirth

* * *

The First Street Church Romances

Sweet and wholesome small town love stories with the community church at their center make for the perfect feel-good reads!

Love's Prayer

Love's Promise

Love's Prophet

Love's Vow

Love's Trial

Love's Treasure

Love's Testament

Love's Gift

* * *

The Alaska Sunrise Romances

These quick, light-hearted romances will put a smile on

your face and a song in your heart. It's time to indulge in a sweet Alaskan get-away!

Must Love Music

Must Love Military

Must Love Mistletoe

Must Love Mutts

Must Love Mommy

Must Love Moo

Must Love Mustangs

Must Love Miracles

Must Love Mermaids

Must Love Movie Star

* * *

The Church Dogs of Charleston

A very special litter of Chihuahua puppies born on Christmas day is adopted by the local church and immediately set to work as tiny therapy dogs.

Little Loves

Mini Miracles

Dainty Darlings

Tiny Treasures

Bitty Blessings

* * *

The Memory Ranch Romances

This new Sled Dogs-spinoff series harnesses the restorative power of both horses and love at Elizabeth Jane's therapeutic memory ranch.

Memories of Home

Memories of Heaven

Memories of Healing

* * *

The Finding Mr. Happily Ever After Series

One bride, four possible grooms, unlimited potential for disaster to strike. Is the man waiting at the end of the aisle the one that's meant to be Jazz's forever love?

Nathan

Chase

Xavier

Edwin

The Finale

* * *

Stand-Alone Novels and Novellas

Whether climbing ladders in the corporate world or taking care of things at home, every woman has a story to tell.

Angels in Our Lives

A Mother's Love

A Colorful Life

* * *

Special Collections & Boxed Sets

From light-hearted comedies to stories about finding hope in the darkest of times, these special boxed editions offer a great way to catch up or to fall in love with Melissa Storm's books for the first time.

Small Town Beginnings: A Series Starter Set

The Sled Dog Series: Books 1-5

The First Street Church Romances: Books 1-3

The Alaska Sunrise Romances: Books 1-5

Finding Mr. Happily Ever After: Books 1-5

True Love Eternal: The 1950's Collection

ABOUT THE AUTHOR

Melissa Storm is a mother first, and everything else second. Writing is her way of showing her daughter just how beautiful life can be, when you pay attention to the everyday wonders that surround us. So, of course, Melissa's USA Today bestselling fiction is highly personal and often based on true stories.

Melissa loves books so much, she married fellow author Falcon Storm. Between the two of them, there are always plenty of imaginative, awe-inspiring stories to share. Melissa and Falcon also run a number of book-related businesses together, including LitRing, Sweet Promise Press, Novel Publicity, Your Author Engine, and the Author Site. When she's not reading, writing, or child-rearing, Melissa spends time relaxing at home in the company of a seemingly unending quantity of dogs and a rescue cat named Schrödinger.

GET IN TOUCH!
www.MelStorm.com
author@melstorm.com

Made in the USA
Columbia, SC
11 December 2018